PAWTRAYAL

THE SPELLWOOD WITCHES, BOOK 5

MELANIE SNOW

Spirit Paw Press, LLC

CONTENTS

The Spellwood Witches Series

Witch's Tail
Howl Play
Tail of a Feather
Impawsible Mischief
Pawtrayal

Pawtrayal

The Spellwood Witches, Book 5

ASIN: B08RCRKKJZ

ISBN: 978-0-578-83991-2

(Spirit Paw Press, LLC, Concord, NH 03303)

www.wendyvandepoll.com/melanie-snow

Thank You

Download Your Free Gift

A Welcome to Witchland Map

Thank you for purchasing *Pawtrayal, The Spellwood Witches, Book 5*. To show my appreciation and because of a popular request from my readers
I am offering a:

Welcome to Witchland Map

https://wendyvandepoll.com/melaniesnowgift

CHAPTER ONE

THE BEAR SAT ON HIS HAUNCHES. THROUGH THE leafy trees, he could see Sarah Spellwood moving about her warmly lit kitchen and stirring something in a pot. The aroma of food wafted toward him, making him salivate. He figured he might just have to rifle through her trash bin later in hopes of finding some leftovers. But then he hung his head, knowing he couldn't. Mournful memories of his distant cousin, trapped and taken to a town far from Witchland for the same offense, filled his mind. Humans discarded food to rot in their bins and then fiercely protected their trash; it made no sense, but the bear had realized long ago that he could never fully comprehend humans.

The bear was glad that Sarah Spellwood was safe for another day, her magic free to grow stronger. But he still had to watch over her, for while she was fierce in her lynx, wolf, crow, and fox spirit magic, she was a relatively young witch, and a prime target of the dark forces because of her powerful Spellwood ancestry. She was also primarily stuck inside a fragile human body. There were so many dangers lurking, and others out to get her. She needed someone, something, to watch over her.

Then the bear observed the man, Sarah's mate, standing up to press his face into hers the way humans liked to do. He liked that man; he sensed that he would always protect Sarah and make her happy. She always seemed to smile more when he was near.

Sarah ladled the vegan spaghetti sauce over a plate of noodles. For the past year, in addition to studying magic, she had also been brushing up on her cooking skills, which had been sadly lacking. This dish actually seemed to turn out well, to her pleasant surprise.

Eli Strongheart observed her cooking uneasily from the kitchen table, where Addie, Sarah's trusty golden-collie mix, lay snoozing at his feet. The last time Sarah had cooked, she nearly cut off her finger because she wasn't paying attention. "That smells good," he finally commented, standing up to kiss her. He glanced at the pot of spaghetti, assessing the beautiful creation the love of his life conjured up.

Sarah beamed up at him. "I perfected this sauce the other day. I've been practicing. I am finding that I love the craft of cooking. It makes me feel very witchy. Now let's eat." She dished up the spaghetti, and Addie moved to stand next to her, begging.

"You know I hate it when you beg." Sarah sighed.

"I can't help it! It's making my mouth water!" Addie shot back.

"At least pretend you're a normal dog with manners?" Sarah requested.

Addie looked forlorn, but complied by returning to her spot at the foot of the dining table.

Sarah and Eli tucked into their food. Eli hesitantly raised the first forkful to his mouth, testing it with the tip of his tongue, then murmured with appreciation when he realized it tasted pretty good. He nodded approvingly at Sarah and began to chow down. Sarah beamed, proud of herself.

As they finished their meal and talked about their respective days, Sarah realized that she loved this little life they had. It was these simple, unexciting moments that made her realize how lucky she truly was. There wasn't a single thing she loathed about Eli. Everything was peaceful and easy. Remarkably easy. They either agreed or talked out their differences and reached a solution. They didn't argue; they didn't dither. They spent most of their time in an easy, peaceful, companionable contentment—enjoying every day, every date, and every inside joke.

She started to run the dishwater in the sink while Eli cleared the dishes. He stood beside her as they washed the dishes together, occasionally flicking soapy water at each other and laughing. The kitchen was so small that they constantly bumped into each other whenever they tried to do anything in it.

Technically Michael Howler's house was all Sarah's, but she shared it with Eli almost every night, and she loved that. An idea suddenly occurred to Sarah: *I wonder if Eli would want to move in with me?*

It seemed crazy that she had not thought of it before. They spent nearly every night together and ate almost every meal together, so what was the point of paying two separate housing bills? After all, Eli still had to pay rent on his tiny place, as well as utilities. In addition, there was the inconvenience of deciding where to sleep each night and packing items to take to his place, or him packing items to bring to hers. They had both left clothes and essentials in each other's homes, but it seemed a bit ridiculous at this point to keep switching back and forth.

But how do I ask? she then thought. *What if he says*

no or freaks out? The men I know hate rushing into things.

"Why would he say no?" Addie piped up, filling Sarah's mind with her telepathic voice.

Sarah smiled down at Addie. *"Would you like him to live with us?"* she responded.

"Absolutely! I love Eli!" Addie answered. To emphasize her point, she hopped up and began to bark excitedly and wag her tail.

"What is it, girl?" Eli asked her, petting her back.

She sat down and looked at him adoringly.

"Want to go for a walk?" Eli asked.

She hopped up again, barking frantically with joy. Eli and Sarah smiled at each other and held hands as they accompanied Addie into the woods for a short evening walk.

The next day, Sarah went to the meeting at Town Hall.

"Hello, guys," Sarah greeted the three mayors of Witchland, Hua, Roger, and Malorie. It had been with her help that they had resolved political conflict and division within the town to install three mayors, all of whom worked together to bring about the best for the town and its surrounding forest.

"Hi, Sarah," Hua said brightly. Hua was Sarah's

next-door neighbor and witch mentor. An herbal witch, she and her wife, Margaret, ran the town's biggest greenhouse and produced many magical herbs and potions.

Malorie's lips curved into her usual mischievous, foxy grin. "Boy, are you going to jump over the moon and back. We've got something very special to discuss with everyone." Malorie was secretly an animal shapeshifter like Sarah, but while Sarah could turn into a wolf, Malorie was a fox who could turn into a human. The two women shared a special connection, since the fox was one of Sarah's spirit animals—her most recently acquired one, in fact. They also had professional mindsets that bonded them ethically and practically; while Sarah was a real estate attorney, Malorie ran several Airbnbs in the town, as well as a traditional New England bed and breakfast, and she had recently opened a restaurant with a partner, Landon. Landon handled the cooking while Malorie handled the business aspects.

"Really?" Sarah grew excited. Few other people had turned up for the town meeting that particular day, but they also looked thrilled to hear the new proposal.

Roger opened the meeting by announcing, "We're now in communication with the New Hampshire governor about making *all* of our forest protected state land, not just Mount Katribus." Roger was a balding, seemingly hapless man, but his passion for the environment paralleled Sarah's. He had originally proposed the idea to acquire the virgin forestland lying on the other side of Mount Katribus, which was previously vulnerable to developers and companies seeking mineral rights.

"Yes!" cried Daisy, standing up to clap. Daisy's red lipstick added a charming glow to her cappuccino skin, and her long dreadlocks danced as she stood up. As the owner of the town's apothecary, she was as zany as she was kind and knowledgeable.

Another voice cheered, and Sarah smiled. It was Michael. She felt him clap her on the back, and then his hand passed through her body with a strange electric zap. Her hair stood on end. Addie wagged her tail, happy to see her former person.

After the meeting concluded, Sarah said goodbye to Michael and jaunted to Javacadabra with her fellow Wolf Coven sisters, Hua, Margaret, Daisy, and Frida. Addie followed along, knowing she was welcome in the cozy coffee shop across from Daisy's apothecary despite the health codes that determined no pets were allowed in eating establishments.

"I trust you guys had a victory?" Susie said cheerfully as she began to whip up their regular orders.

Her white cat, Zeva, purred and surveyed them through sleepy half-slit eyes. *A victory indeed. I can tell*," Zeva told Sarah telepathically. Only Susie and Sarah could hear Zeva.

"And what a victory," Daisy said happily, slapping the tabletop.

"No more Levi Gonforth associates coming around!" Margaret cheered. Then her face darkened momentarily as she thought of the sleazy real estate attorney and his greedy developer associates.

"That's our hope, to keep people like that out for good. It's not for sure yet, though," Hua cautioned. "The governor may veto our proposal in favor of the tax profits he could make from opening up the forest to development."

"True," Sarah said, her stomach sinking. "But we all know our own mettle. We won't stand for such a thing."

"We're pretty good at kicking developer types out." Frida laughed, also recalling the various times Sarah and the other witches had used magic to drive out undesirable people with bad intentions for the town. "We can always resort to our old ways, if we can't make this a legally binding thing."

Sarah cracked a grin. "I did rather enjoy stalking that poacher Lester as a wolf and scaring him so badly that he never came back," she said. "That man tried so hard to be intimidating, but nobody beats a witch that can shapeshift into a wolf!"

All of the witches laughed. Their magical powers were a secret they kept safe as they did what they could to defend Witchland from modern evils.

"And how is Eli doing?" Daisy asked, a kind but teasing tone in her voice.

A huge smile spread across Sarah's face. She always smiled when she thought of him, without even thinking about it. "Good, very good." She set her tea latte down and swallowed. "Actually, I'm thinking of asking him to move in with me."

"That's a big step," Frida commented.

Sarah looked at her, wondering if she was hinting about a premonition. Out of anyone, Sarah trusted Frida's advice about the future the most. But Frida was always frustratingly opaque, insisting that people follow their hearts regarding the future instead of dispensing specific advice to them. "Do you think it's a bad move?" Sarah asked.

"It is up to your heart's voice," Frida replied, smiling.

Sarah tried her best to suppress her eye roll and groan of frustration.

"When you're ready, you're ready," Hua said softly, looking adoringly at her wife. Margaret smiled back, undoubtedly thinking back to whenever they had first made the step to cohabitate, back in their younger years in Manhattan.

"I would . . . wait," Frida piped up.

Sarah swiveled to face Frida head-on. "Really?" she asked, her interest piqued.

"I know it's old-fashioned, and I don't agree, but when I was younger, we were taught to always let the man take the lead when it comes to these kinds of things," Frida replied.

"No, this is the age of female empowerment, as you know," Daisy argued. "The time has come for women to take the lead now!"

"And that's why Earl went off chasing dragons," Frida shot back playfully.

Daisy and Frida often liked to joke about the warlock they had both loved, and who had left them behind in Witchland to hunt dragons in Wales.

"Oh, you shush your mouth," Daisy teased back.

Sarah groaned. "I just don't know. I don't think he'll ever ask. I mean, we've been together for quite a while. And it's frustrating, paying double the bills and splitting time between our places, when we spend every night together anyway."

"Maybe he is thinking about it, too, or something similar," Daisy commented. She had a strange twinkle in her eye, as if she knew something.

Sarah surveyed Daisy, trying to decipher the meaning behind her expression, when Hua distracted her. "What are you going to do with Michael's old house?"

"Well, I'd hoped Eli would move in with me there," Sarah responded. "That's my office, and I see a lot of my clients there, so it would be odd to move."

"It's a bit cramped for two, don't you think?" Margaret mused.

"Well . . . maybe." Sarah thought uncomfortably of waking up nearly falling off the twin bed when Eli slept over, or piling the clothes that didn't fit in the tiny closet in boxes that she stored under the bed. And last night, while making spaghetti, she had had to chop the veggies in the sink due to the lack of counter space. "But his place isn't much better," she added.

"There's a cute little yellow cottage for rent near my house. A one-bedroom, but much roomier than Michael's place," Frida said. "Go talk to Jan at the realty office and see how much rent is. I doubt it's unreasonable."

Sarah smiled. "Well, if he agrees to move in together, maybe a new place would be the best bet. I could keep Michael's house as my office."

"There you go," Hua said.

"I created a new tea," Daisy changed the subject. "It changes your hair color. Would you ladies like to test it out?"

The women laughingly agreed. They tasted the tea

from a bottle Daisy kept in her purse and laughed as their hair began to change from pink to blue to green.

A tourist, who was munching on a cookie a few tables away, stopped eating to stare with his jaw hanging. "I guess this is why they call it Witchland," he finally mumbled, shaking his head in bewilderment.

Once the effect had faded, Sarah went home to change for a date with Eli. They were going out of town to try a new Indian restaurant in Hanover. Eli knew the owners.

As she reached her door, she paused to admire the little cottage she had lived in for the past two years. She loved this place, but it was suffocatingly small at times. She admired the neatness of the silver letters spelling out her name on the door: Sarah Spellwood, Attorney at Law. The view of the flowers in the yard, the way the trees and shrubs clustered close to the house in the back, the hummingbirds that visited the feeder she hung in front of the window over her desk. Back in New York, where the view from her desk was a bleak gray building across the street, she had never imagined having such a magical office or home. But maybe now it was time to move on and make this little place just an office. Combining work and home sometimes felt too chaotic.

"Do you even think Eli wants this?" she asked

Addie, thinking of how weird Daisy had acted during the conversation about moving in with him.

"*Of course,*" Addie said. "*He loves you so much.*"

"But he has never brought it up—not even once. And he seems pretty content with his little house. I mean, maybe he likes having his own space?" Sarah mused.

"*Just ask him,*" Addie said. Then she sighed, happily. "*I'm so glad we dogs don't need to worry about these things.*"

"Right, Kelvin just visits whenever he pleases." Sarah rolled her eyes. "That wolf is eating me out of house and home. Where has he been the past few days, anyway?"

"*He says he smelled some animal in the woods and wanted to investigate, so he hasn't come around,*" Addie replied. Sarah envied how carefree Addie was about her love life with the handsome, sarcastic Kelvin, a wild wolf from the forest. Addie certainly didn't have to obsess over asking Kelvin questions or forming their future. She just let things be.

Maybe that's how I need to be with Eli. Just let things be. Let him take the lead, like Frida suggested, she thought. *But that is so old-fashioned.*

"*You're still obsessing,*" Addie commented.

Sarah froze, her hand on the doorknob. Through the thick green canopy of forest beyond her house, she thought she saw a lumbering shadow shift. But when she looked more closely, there was nothing there.

Addie suddenly perked up, her nose to the air. *"There it is!"* she cried triumphantly.

"What is it?" Sarah demanded.

"That animal Kelvin is tracking!" Addie barked and lunged at the woods, but Sarah called her back.

"What kind of animal is it?" Sarah asked.

"I don't know what it's called! Musky! Male! Thick fur!"

"Just leave it alone. It will reveal itself to us when it wants to," she told Addie, who was trembling with excitement and the desire to chase. "Maybe it's my fifth spirit animal," Sarah added hopefully. Sarah had already met and acquired the other four animals: the wolf, the lynx, the crow, and the fox. But there were supposed to be two more animals in her spirit animal team, and they had yet to reveal themselves.

CHAPTER TWO

SARAH MET WITH HER COVEN SISTERS AT Javacadabra the next morning to begin another witch lesson. While she was a fairly practiced and confident witch now, her sisters had decided to start teaching her "the good stuff." Sarah was beyond excited. These were the complicated spells she had been waiting to learn since she had first discovered—or rather, rediscovered—her powers upon moving to Witchland.

"Well, we are going to start with a powerful energetic tracking spell today," Daisy began. "It is critical for finding out who was where, and why. You can practically read the thoughts of a person or animal who passed through an area just by observing its energetic trail."

"I can track a bit," Sarah said.

"But the spell I'm about to show you is much stronger," Daisy said.

The other witches followed Daisy and Sarah out into a small patch of trees near the center of the town square. Susie joined, holding Zeva. Though Susie was not necessarily a practicing witch or a member of the Wolf Coven, she loved watching them at work.

The energetic trails of many dogs, humans, and other creatures mingled there, making it a challenging site for clear tracking. Daisy commanded Sarah to clear her mind and then recite a spell for otherworldly vision, which Sarah was able to do almost effortlessly. Immediately, the ground in front of her turned into a maze of crisscrossing, glowing blue trails.

"Now focus on a single one," Daisy instructed.

Sarah picked a random trail and honed in on it with her whole being. Immediately, the trail's energy began to swirl in her spirit, and she felt as if she were someone else. Her nose was full of the scent of cherry lip balm, and a mosquito bite itched on the back of her calf, though Sarah herself was not wearing lip balm and didn't have such a bite. She realized that she was fully following the trail as the other person. After focusing on the energetic sensations for a moment, she realized that she was following the path of Alex, the town clerk.

Sarah beamed, proud of her own progress, as she

turned her attention to other energetic trails. A year or two ago, she had to struggle to enter the state of mind that allowed her to become one with plants and animals and speak with them. At the very beginning, she could only hear Addie when the Leekins were nearby. But now she could slip into that state of mind necessary for magic without trying.

She let the energy flow into her and clearly sensed the path where the grocer had walked by with his greyhound that morning, and the slightly more faded path of Susan Lake, the town's former interim mayor, carrying a basket of baked bread from the bakery soon after it had opened first thing in the morning. Sarah didn't see or smell the energy, but rather felt it pervade her whole being, giving her a sensation of almost being one with the people who had traversed the square.

Daisy then taught her a short spell to recite that gave her a more laser-focused view of each individual trail.

> *First sight, Second Sight, All sight,*
> *Come to me now. With this light,*
> *Make my psychic being open*
> *As this spell is spoken.*

Sarah was stunned by how much more she could feel from the trails of energy now. The grocer had been thinking about how to apologize to his wife, since he had forgotten their anniversary the night before; Susan Lake had been contentedly contemplating which travel trailer to buy to make a cross-country road trip to meet up with her daughter in Southern California; Alex had been thinking about her night before with Landon . . . Sarah blushed and quickly removed herself from that trail.

"See how everything and everyone in life mingles energetically? It makes it quite easy—and effective—to track people," Daisy explained. "You can learn everything that someone is feeling, thinking, doing. Their intentions, their circumstances."

"Be careful, though," Frida cautioned suddenly. She looked doubtful of this lesson. "Without proper training in clearing, you tend to absorb too much. Other people's problems become your own. It's called sympathetic empathy, and it can be a nightmare if you don't know how to control it, how to filter it out." She stepped closer to Sarah. "And you can also absorb the dark energies of people or things, as well as places where tragic events have happened. Those things can stay with you forever and haunt you if you don't clear them out."

Sarah turned off her empathic sensing and faced Frida. "I think I know what you mean. At times, I can still feel the malignant energy surrounding Madras when we fought on top of Mount Katribus. How do I cleanse and protect myself?"

Frida nodded. "Sarah, this spell will help you absolve yourself of guilt from sinister energies and clear your essence from feeling responsible," said Frida.

> *Take note of what brings me down to banish,*
> *The guilt I have will therefore vanish,*
> *I will not allow it to steer me back,*
> *This heavy energy will not take me off track.*

As soon as Sarah began to chant the spell, she felt the residual energy from her empathic tracking fade away and disappear altogether. She felt clean, whole, as if her soul had taken a hot shower. "I think I need to practice this in a more negative situation, though. The energy I was just tracking was pretty light," she pointed out, wondering if this spell would be powerful enough in situations where she came face to face with true evil. Though Madras had been gone for almost two years, Sarah always tried to be prepared for another encounter with her.

"Of course," Frida acquiesced. "Come to think of it, there is a perfect place for you to practice. There is a historic house near my parlor where a murder happened three decades ago. It has never been sold, and the house sits abandoned. It feels very forlorn, very . . ."

"Creepy?" Sarah suggested.

"Yes, absolutely. The house still holds the energy of the violence that occurred there, as well as the pain and confusion of the ghost. He doesn't act very friendly or receptive to me, so I haven't really spoken with him. But I can tell he wants his murder to be solved."

Sarah felt her heart start to beat faster. *Is this a new case?* She glanced at Addie, who wagged her tail and asked, "*Are we going to solve this one, Sarah?*"

"*We just might.*" Sarah winked.

Frida gestured for the witches to follow her to the house.

As they strolled through the town, taking in the fragrance of the flowers clustered along the richly shaded streets, Frida explained how she often worked as a medium for ghosts left behind after sudden or unpleasant deaths. "They usually only stay when they sense they have a job to do. They can't cross over yet. They want justice, or they want to ensure a family member doesn't steal their estate if they didn't leave a will, or they want to tell everyone they love goodbye. My job is to help transmit their messages to their loved ones and bring peace to everyone," she explained.

"I always admired that type of work. Very painful," Margaret said.

"It can be. I encounter some horrible things. But the work itself is quite rewarding. Sometimes, I am even able to get the ghost to cross over and bring closure to everyone." Frida smiled as she recounted the tale of an old man who wanted revenge against his wife and neighbor, who had started seeing one another after he died. "She waited a year, mind you. It wasn't a huge scandal. But he was so angry! He would slam doors, throw things across the room, and whisper in her ear while she was sleeping to scare her. The angry ghosts are the hardest ones to placate, and the hardest ones to remove. They can create a lot of drama with their rage, and that rage can attract much darker entities into the space as well."

"Like demons?" Sarah inquired.

"Exactly. Or, as you remember from before, anger in Levi Gonforth's heart let Madras in. There are sometimes stronger, angrier ghosts who will take advantage of these situations to work out their own agendas. The bad energy invites them in." Frida sighed. "This particular situation I'm talking about was turning into a very ugly haunting. But I conducted a séance with everyone, and the poor ghost and his wife were able to say goodbye. The ghost realized he just wanted her to be happy, and he moved on. His wife also realized that she hadn't memorialized him properly because it hurt too much, so she gave him a shrine

21

over the fireplace, and that made him happy. That event was enough to wash the residual angry energy from the house, and she and her new husband were able to live there happily ever after."

"What about when the residual energy remains, like in the house we're visiting?" Hua asked. As an herbal witch, she was not familiar with Frida's type of magic, either.

Frida sighed again. "If someone hires me, I can usually cleanse the bad energy out, more or less. But residual energy is like a memory imprinted on the people and objects affected by the energetic event. And you know that you can't just make yourself forget something; there's a good reason why you remember painful events, so that you learn from them. It's the same with energetic imprints. Some things—like the trails you were just tracking in the square, Sarah—tend to fade very quickly because they don't carry much weight to anyone involved. Other times, they have a lot of emotional power—for example, violence or joy—so they stay for a long time. Sometimes, there is little one can do to cleanse such energetic imprints.

"In the case of this house, it's really not my concern, so I have left it alone. Sadness, despair, and anger all have a place in this world, too, or else we wouldn't be able to appreciate joy and love." Frida then stopped walking before an old, shuttered Victorian-

style house with a sagging balcony. A red 'No Tres-
passing: Private Property' sign was nailed into the
once-grand oak doors.

Immediately, Sarah could sense the forlorn and
rather creepy energetic imprint that Frida had
mentioned. The house felt cold and unhappy. But the
feeling did not arise so much from the murder that had
happened there, Sarah realized; it was the house itself,
feeling neglected and abandoned, wondering why it
couldn't be a source of the comfort, security, and love
for someone.

Sarah drew in a sharp intake of breath. "The house
just wants to be loved and lived in again," she said
softly.

She envisioned fixing up that balcony, replacing
the shattered windowpane in the bay window, and
planting gloriously bright pansies along the walkway to
the porch. She imagined turning the walls of peeling,
graying paint to happy yellow, with light green trim. A
greenhouse in the back, to keep them sustained with
vegetables and seasoning herbs all winter long. The
wild, tangled rosebushes in the front were so over-
grown that only a few blooms were visible; she imagined trimming them into neat shapes, fertilizing them,
and watching rich dark pink blooms bursting forth
from among the leaves and thorns come May.

She walked up to the gorgeous maple tree standing

like a lord over the yard and placed a loving hand on its trunk, wondering how long it had been since anyone had bothered to admire the tree or trim its gnarled branches. The tree shook a few of its leaves at her in greeting; she could sense that it had a boisterous spirit. Some teenagers had carved their initials in the trunk with a pocketknife and dated them 1972.

"Maybe it does want to be fixed up, but who would want to live in a house where a murder took place?" Margaret asked. Then she stopped talking, her eyes widening, as she realized Sarah had been living in Michael's house this whole time, sleeping in the very room where he had been bludgeoned and pushed down the stairs to his end.

"I think some TLC would be all this house needs to feel good again," Sarah told her, choosing not to dwell on the pain of Michael's murder. "Michael's house used to scare me, but it doesn't anymore. In fact, I like being there because I can feel close to him, even when his ghost isn't around." She turned back to the house, smiling dotingly. "Do you know who owns it?"

"I'm sure you can find out in the library," Frida suggested. "I don't have the foggiest clue. No one has lived here for quite some time."

"Are you thinking of buying it for yourself?" Hua gasped. Then she grinned. "Ooh, I know why!"

"I knew there was a reason I wanted to take you

here." Frida grinned. "That's another way to block out and cleanse bad energy—hear the bad energy, understand it, give it a voice, then make something good out of it. Things like love and fresh paint can help lift negativity and energetic ugliness from houses." She proudly adjusted her feathered shawl while Daisy rolled her eyes, forever annoyed by Frida's boasting. "Ah, something told me to bring you here. I just connected you with your dream house!"

"You can't say you knew what would happen after the fact," Daisy grumbled.

"I never said I knew what would happen. But I let the universe guide me, and here we are," Frida shot back. "The universe is never wrong, and I'm simply an agent of its will."

Daisy rolled her eyes again. "Aren't we all?"

Frida was clearly thinking of a smart comeback, but ultimately, she just smiled sweetly and agreed, "Yes, we all are."

Though the two women were close friends and coven sisters now, they still had some moments of rivalry. The other witches simply ignored their brief, annoying spats.

Sarah stared up at the house one last time. This place was just the right size for her and Eli . . . They could even get a California King mattress and stop fighting over the covers!

Just then, a sharp voice intruded into her mind. *"And what the hell makes you think that you can just move in and repaint my house?"*

Sarah's hairs stood up on end. *"Hello,"* she telepathically reached out to the ghost. *"What's your name?"* She understood that ghosts often felt left out of life and mournful of their own deaths, so treating them like normal people really mattered to them.

But this ghost was still petulant. *"I'm the guy who will make your life hell if you move in here and start changing things! I like them the way they are! Stay the hell out!"* he growled.

"What's your name?" Sarah asked again.

"Arnold Packington! The guy who owns this place?" he snapped.

"I think it belongs to someone else now," she gently told him. *"Maybe an heir of yours?"*

But that only seemed to enrage Arnold more. Suddenly, a sharp rock hurtled out of nowhere and hit Sarah's shin. Sarah cried out and bent down to rub the bruise. Addie growled at the ghost, her hackles standing up straight, warning him not to hurt her person.

"That ghost doesn't seem to like you," Hua commented uneasily. "Maybe we should leave."

Sarah agreed, but she kept looking over her shoulder back at the house.

CHAPTER THREE

AFTER SAYING GOODBYE TO HER COVEN SISTERS and thanking them for the insightful lesson, Sarah picked up a couple of sandwiches for Eli and his faithful deputy, Jenna Mora, the town's paranormal gatekeeper. She was in charge of keeping malevolent spirits out of Witchland.

"You're the best girlfriend ever." Eli grinned when Sarah appeared with the food. "And you brought my favorite! Chicken salad with cranberry." Though Sarah was a vegan, Eli only ate vegan food when he dined with her. He still had his penchant for meat.

"Thanks." Jenna grinned, accepting her sandwich. "I'm hungry enough to eat a bear."

Sarah grimaced at the reference. She was still waiting to meet the bear, who had been her fifth animal oracle drawn by Frida and, therefore, was to be her fifth animal spirit guide. She sat on the corner of Eli's desk and watched him fill out forms while munching on his sandwich.

"So, why didn't you ever tell me about the Arnold Packington cold case?" she asked nonchalantly.

Eli glanced up at her. "Oh, wow, that hasn't crossed my mind in a while. Way before my time."

"Mine, too, but I remember hearing about it growing up," Jenna piped up. "We still get calls about kids breaking in there on Halloween because it's haunted."

"What happened exactly?" Sarah was practically salivating at the thought of a fresh mystery.

Addie wagged her tail from her position at Sarah's feet. *"Get all of the juicy details,"* Addie urged her.

"Oh, evidently he was stabbed in his home. Police had several suspects, but no evidence to take any of them to court. No witnesses, no murder weapon, nothing." Eli frowned. "I'd have to read the case file to freshen my memory."

"Any chance I could borrow that case file?" Sarah asked. Seeing the shadow of doubt crossing Eli's face, she jokingly clutched her hands in front of her chest and began to beg, "Pretty please?"

"You know I could get in trouble." Eli sighed. "It's mishandling of case files and evidence."

"But I'm not sure anyone would find out if I just

happened to have the case file lying on my desk, and you swiped it when I wasn't looking," Jenna proposed.

Sarah flashed her a huge grin. "See? Jenna gets it. She gets I'm practically one of the Witchland cops."

Eli sighed, but smiled. "I love seeing you all worked up about a mystery. If anyone has a chance of solving it, it would be you. And Addie." He leaned down to scratch Addie behind the ears.

Jenna grinned and headed back to the filing room. Sarah was shocked at how thin the file was when Jenna returned and placed it on the corner of her desk. After Sarah grabbed it and stashed it in her book bag, she kissed Eli and said, "Are you coming over tonight?"

"I was planning on it," he said. "Unless you want to come over to my place?"

"Why don't you two just move in together already? My boyfriend and I already have," Jenna asked.

Sarah squirmed. She tried to read Eli's face to see how he felt about it. But he seemed to be simply waiting for her response.

"Uh, well, either way, I think I have to go to that house where Arnold died and speak to him for a while," Sarah said. "So I'll be home late. You can just let yourself in."

"Sure thing." Eli pecked her lips a final time and returned to his paperwork.

Sarah said goodbye to Jenna and headed home to immerse herself in the case file.

The thin file yielded a pathetically small amount of information. There were the bloody crime scene photos, a few unmatched fingerprints lifted from the doorknob, and the autopsy report. There was also a single newspaper clipping referring to the crime and asking for information. Apparently, the only person to call in was an anonymous lady; she claimed that Arnold was in possession of a large treasure and that he was probably killed over that. In an infuriatingly brief police report, an Officer Thomas wrote that his team swept the house again to follow up on the lead, but they did not find any evidence of a treasure—or any sort of robbery, for that matter.

There were also a few brief, fruitless interviews with people who knew Arnold, none of whom were able to name anyone who would want him dead. One thing that stood out to Sarah was that one of Arnold's friends, a Stuart Lincoln, stated that Arnold was "very interested in treasure hunting."

"Hmm, treasure again," Sarah remarked to Addie. "This is all very strange. Why would a man just randomly be stabbed to death, especially in this peaceful town? I wonder if the treasure lead wasn't such a dead end after all."

"*Are you ready to go talk to him and get his side of the story?*" Addie asked eagerly.

Sarah stood on the creaky steps of the abandoned house.

"*Arnold? Mr. Packington?*" she called telepathically.

Though no one answered, Sarah sensed Arnold's presence. He did not seem particularly warm or welcoming.

"*Listen. I heard about your murder. And I like to solve mysteries. What do you say you let me solve yours?*" Sarah continued.

There was only eerie silence.

"*I know you must be suffering, wondering who killed you and why . . . Or do you know who did it?*" The idea occurred to Sarah that the police had never interviewed Arnold's ghost, for they didn't have a witch on their team in 1992. *Forensic witchcraft,* Sarah thought with a giggle.

"*If I knew who did it, don't you think I'd have crossed over already?*" a cranky voice finally answered.

"*So you don't know? It's been unsolved for nearly thirty years. Why don't we work on resolving it and letting you rest in peace?*" Sarah pushed on.

31

"*Look, my murder may just be some novelty for your girly hobby to help you pass the time, but it's deeply personal to me. I want it handled by profession-als,*" he replied with deep irritation in his voice. "*So move along, and leave me alone! And don't touch my house!*"

Sarah sighed. "*Okay, but I have already solved two murders in this town, and a series of thefts. I'm a pretty good sleuth, actually, and so is my dog. I also have a whole coven of witches behind me to lend me aid when I need it. If anybody has a chance of cracking your cold case, it's us.*"

Arnold was silent. Then he began to materialize before Sarah. He appeared to be in his mid-forties and had thinning brown hair and a still-healthy brown mustache and beard. There were bloodstains and open stab wounds on the front of his plaid shirt, which glowed darker than his ghostly aura. He reminded Sarah of a mountain man, someone who might only come to town occasionally to stock up on supplies. Judging by his weathered tan skin and rough hands, he evidently did spend a lot of time outdoors.

"Well, look at you, a Spellwood trying to solve my case," he said. There was no more malice or annoyance in his voice. In fact, Sarah could detect a slight thrill of excitement. "You know, your aunt Beth never did pay me any mind. I tried taking her out once, but she wanted nothing to do with me." He laughed, no bitterness in his reminiscing. "At first I was pretty angry; I thought she just wanted a younger guy, you know, because I was quite a bit older than her. But then I realized she didn't want anything to do with men, period! She was a witch, through and through! Dedicated entirely to her craft."

Sarah smiled warmly. "I really loved my aunt. She was a great witch."

Arnold looked Sarah up and down. "Well, you can call me Arnie. I can't object to Beth's niece looking into my case for me, I guess." Sadness crinkled his face. "Nobody has touched that thing since, oh, I would say '94."

"I'm sorry," Sarah said compassionately. She sat on the steps and pulled out his case file from her book bag. Then she opened a notebook and uncapped a pen. "Can I get some details from you? Can you tell me what really happened that day?"

Arnie shut his eyes. "It had to do with my treasure, that's for sure."

"Treasure?" Sarah asked, pleased that her hunch about the anonymous lady's lead was right.

"Yes. I found it in Nevada, a Spanish conquistador's treasure. Gold, rubies, emeralds, pearls, you name it. Worth millions. You see, my father was a treasure hunter, and he raised me to be the same. Well, some of my friends were pretty astute treasure hunters, and they wanted it, too. They realized I must have gotten to it, and they started circling, you know, asking questions. They were insulted I wouldn't share the treasure with them. I knew someone was going to steal it, so I buried it in the woods."

Sarah's eyes widened, and she made a note to herself on the margins of her notebook: *Could this be the treasure Malorie found??? Talk to Malorie!!*

"So your murder was probably connected to the treasure, but you don't know who did it? You didn't see anything, hear anything, any valuable clues?"

He shrugged haplessly. "It was one of my treasure-hunting buddies, that's for sure. But I didn't recognize who it was. The guy was average height, dressed all in black, his face, hands, and hair covered. He came in the night and attacked me in my bed. We fought and fell down the stairs, right onto the foyer there." He pointed at the door, implying the foyer lay on the other side. "And he kept screaming, 'Where is it, Arnie? Where is it?' He was using some kind of fake voice; I didn't recognize it. He smelled like . . . like Vaseline and whisky. I didn't see anything at all. Just that his eyes were very, very shiny, but it was so dark I couldn't see the color.

"Then he took a knife from his belt and threatened me with it. He told me he didn't want to kill me, but he needed me to show him where the treasure was. Well, I wrestled the knife away from him and almost stabbed him in self-defense, when he got the better of me and stabbed me five times. As I was bleeding, he said if I told him where the treasure was, then he would take me to the hospital. I tried, but I was so weak I couldn't speak. Some noise scared him, and he panicked and ran off with the knife."

"I'm so sorry," Sarah murmured when his tale concluded. She shook her head and began to write down the details, asking him for clarification about where exactly he was at each part of the night. Arnie simply told her he couldn't give her much more detail because it was all a terrifying blur to him.

"Did the guy leave any bloody footprints? I don't see any documented in your case," Sarah finally commented.

"I don't know. Because I was on my back, most of the blood pooled directly under and around me. It didn't really get everywhere, just those streaks and spatters on the walls and the stairs. You can see them in the crime scene photos." Arnie pointed at the photos in the file and then shrunk back in horror, clearly disturbed to see the photos of his own dead body.

Sarah gently closed the file to cover the photos. "We will find out who did this to you, Arnie. This was a long time ago, but there is a chance that your killer is still alive, and we will make sure he spends the rest of his life in prison."

Addie barked, *"Let's put him away!"*

"Okay," Arnie said. He sounded happy to hear their promise, but also as if he didn't have too much faith in their ability to track down his murderer. He began to fade away, needing his rest. Ghosts needed far more rest than humans did, and human interactions tended to tire them out.

Walking home from Arnie's house, Sarah called on Michael, her ghostly mentor. When he appeared, Addie jumped on him affectionately, barking in joy. Sarah gave him a hug, even though her arms passed right through him. Then she caught him up on the case and asked his opinion.

"Death makes things blurry. He might not even remember his own murder properly. I'm sure he's missing a lot of things. I certainly was," Michael informed her.

"Well, I think we can fill in the holes," Sarah said hopefully. "Do you want to help?"

"Of course!" Michael crowed. "I love solving mysteries with my two girls!"

CHAPTER FOUR

MALORIE WORE HER FLAMING RED HAIR TIED BACK with a bandana and her sleeves rolled up as she scrubbed a toilet in her bed and breakfast. "These people are unreal in how they mess the place up! These are the same types who go out to the woods and leave their trash everywhere!" she protested to Sarah.

"I'm sorry." Sarah wrinkled her nose at the toilet, glad she had never had to work in hospitality. Her college job at a diner had been unpleasant enough, cleaning up after people. Some people were made for such jobs, but Sarah was not. "Was this worth leaving the forest and becoming a full-time human?" Sarah then joked.

Malorie stopped scrubbing for a second to give Sarah a mock angry look. "Sometimes I seriously consider turning back into a fox and disappearing into those trees, let me tell you."

Sarah laughed. "Well, listen, I've actually come here as part of a mystery I'm solving. It's the mystery of Arnold Packington's murder."

Malorie shrugged, clearly not knowing the story. Sarah filled her in, and Malorie's jaw dropped when she heard mention of the treasure.

"Wow, so he hid a treasure in the woods, huh?" Malorie mused.

"Do you think it was the one you uncovered?" Sarah prodded.

"Might be. I mean, I'm sure there aren't too many buried treasures out there," Malorie agreed.

"Do you remember the spot where the treasure is buried?" Sarah asked.

"Sure. Want me to show you?" Malorie asked.

Sarah followed Malorie deep into the woods. At a nondescript spot that anyone would have overlooked, Malorie stopped. "Well, it was here. I was digging for grubs when I hit the lid of the old steamer trunk it was in. I dug it up, and there was so much gold in there, and jewels, too. I turned into a human, took it to various jewelers and pawnshops, and converted it all to cash. That's how I bought my businesses and managed to make it as a human."

"A traceless human." Sarah nodded, remembering

her background check into Malorie during the mayoral election.

Malorie grinned. "I bet my background just *threw* you and Eli for a loop! You didn't expect me to be a fox, now did you?"

"Not at all," Sarah admitted. "And I wonder if I'll be surprised by who the killer is, as well. They might be right under my nose."

"Someone here in town," Malorie agreed.

"I just need to find out who all of his buddies were," Sarah mused as she began snapping pictures of the spot Malorie had led her to. Then she asked Malorie to excuse her for a moment as she closed her eyes, scanning the area for energy trails.

There were many trails, mostly of animals. She even found an old trail of herself, hiking the area with Addie. She could sense Addie's happiness and her own contentment in that memory. Some of the trails were very old and faint, while others were more vivid and fresh. After a moment, she finally located one, a very old one, that seemed familiar.

She allowed herself to become the trail. She felt like her back was hunched over, and her vision was horrible. There was a slight weight on her shoulder; when she turned her head, she saw a crow.

"Harriet!" Sarah said to Addie.

"What was Harriet doing here?" Addie asked.

"Your guess is as good as mine. Let's confirm that Arnie did bury his treasure here, and then let's interview Harriet," Sarah replied.

Sarah returned to her energetic tracking. As she began to concentrate more, she realized that she detected another powerful and disturbing energetic trail, one that was even older than Harriet's. Something about it seemed disturbingly familiar, and Sarah felt chills run up and down her spine. *Madras,* she thought with horror.

Addie looked at her and whined in fear. She knew what Sarah was feeling because familiars shared such strong empathetic connections with their witches. She was practically experiencing the energetic tracking through her person. The energy was just as familiar to her as it was to Sarah, and just as unwelcome.

"Maybe Madras came here long ago. But how did she know where this was? And how did Harriet also know?" Sarah asked Addie. Then she froze. "You don't think . . . Could Harriet be working with Madras?"

"Maybe! I can't imagine her doing that," Addie said.

"I can hear you guys." Malorie laughed. "Harriet is weird, but I don't know about her working with Madras."

"Only one way to find out," Sarah said grimly.

After hiking back to town with Malorie, during

which they discussed the acquisition of the land behind Mount Katribus and the valley near Blackberry Summit, Sarah thanked her and headed to the haunted house. She gazed up at the Victorian, still entranced by its beauty, before calling to Arnie.

Arnie slowly materialized. "Well?" he asked impatiently.

Sarah showed him the photos on her phone. "Does this look like the spot where you buried the treasure?"

Arnie narrowed his eyes, taking in the details of the photos. Then he grinned and nodded emphatically. "Yes, yes, it is!"

"And it was in an old steamer trunk?" Sarah asked.

"Yes, my dad's old trunk. What—how did you find it?"

Sarah paused, surprised the ghost did not know about Malorie. "You don't watch your treasure?"

"What would be the point? Besides, I don't want to lead someone to it," Arnie replied indignantly.

"Well, then, you don't know that someone found it," Sarah went on. "Not your murderer, by the way."

Arnie stared at her. "Who on earth found it? I hid it very well!"

"Let's just say a forest creature dug it up. Now Malorie Vulpes, one of the town mayors, has it. She used it to fund her businesses," Sarah explained.

Arnie began to tremble with rage. "That crook!

What right does she have to take my treasure and fund her businesses with it?"

"Don't call her that," Sarah chided him. "She's a hardworking businesswoman—maybe call her . . . a business *fox*?" Sarah mused.

"What would you even use the treasure for now?" Addie asked with her characteristic frankness. *"At least it went to something good!"*

Arnie was still shaking as he looked from Sarah to Addie and back again. Then he began to relax, but only slightly. "I had plans, you know, a life. I wanted to do something with that treasure. Heck, just knowing I *had* a treasure mattered a lot to me. Now it's been taken and used by someone else to live her life, and I am still here."

Sarah reached out to place a gentle hand on his shoulder, but her hand passed through him. He shuddered and backed away. "I hate that, being touched. Don't do it. I hate when people and things move right through me."

"Sorry. I won't do it again. Do you think you will be more at peace when I solve this murder?" Sarah asked.

Arnie shrugged unhappily. "I guess we'll see, if you ever solve it." Then he raised his eyes to meet hers. Sarah noticed they were a deep bronze color. "It kind of feels like my death was utterly pointless now, doesn't it? I would honestly feel better if my killer had found the treasure because at least then I wouldn't have died for nothing."

Sarah nodded empathetically. "Well, I did a quick energetic scan of the area, and I can't sense that anyone else was even there but one person. And I intend to talk to her and find out what she knows. It's a lead, if nothing else."

Arnie nodded and thanked her begrudgingly as he began to fade.

Sarah intended to interview Harriet, but when she went by Harriet's hut, it appeared empty. "She's probably on one of her weird forages in the caves," Sarah told Addie, who nodded in agreement. "Maybe she's also hiding because she had a sense we would come to ask her about the murder? Next time I think I'll have to use an invisibility spell."

"Sounds good. For now, let's just go home. I want to see Kelvin. I sense he's at the door," Addie told Sarah.

"I hope to see Eli," Sarah agreed. But just then, as she checked her phone, she got an email from Eli explaining that he would be working late and would probably just stay at his place for the night. She sighed, but she understood. *This is why we should move in together!* she thought.

As soon as they got home, Sarah changed into her biggest sweats and lounged on her porch swing with a glass of iced tea that was garnished with mint from Margaret and Hua's greenhouse. For a few moments, she simply suspended her mind, taking in the pleasing late evening and trying not to dwell on the case too much. This case could keep her up all night, and she needed her rest to perform magic and investigative work at her peak abilities. Self-care had become another crucial element of her magical practice, something she had formerly neglected when she was first learning.

A rustling in the trees beyond her house startled her out of her reverie. She glanced around, but she was unable to see the source of the commotion from her porch. Addie and Kelvin, who were snoozing at her feet, rapidly sprang up and shot around the house. *"It's the creature from the woods with the pungent scent I've been smelling!"* cried Addie excitedly.

"You two stop it!" Sarah commanded.

The two canines paused, still looking at the woods, eager to chase the bear. But they listened to Sarah. Even Kelvin had started to take Sarah's lead at times, knowing that she was a source of food, shelter, and the spell that kept him invisible to humans and hunters. He felt that she was deserving of his trust and respect, though he continued to be wild in nature. Sarah didn't try to tame him, knowing that a wild animal belonged in the wild.

Sarah stepped off her porch and walked toward the woods. She could not see anything in the dim light. Using her phone's flashlight app, she shined a beam into the trees and caught the reflection of two huge eyes glinting back at her. There, partially hidden among the thorny blackberry bushes, was the outline of a large black bear sitting on his haunches. He surveyed her with those glinting eyes, his nose moving rapidly as he took in her scent and that of the canines.

Sarah shut her eyes and reached out with her mind. She felt the bear's reassuring presence, protective and strong, warm and intelligent. He had come as a friend. But he did not seem ready to come near her. There was still a deep sense of reticence and even some fear emanating from his hulking mass.

"Who are you?" she asked him with her mind.

He did not reply. He simply dropped to all fours and ambled away, his large backside immediately disappearing beyond the weak beam of her phone's flashlight app.

"Now can I please chase after him?" Kelvin whined.

"No! He's a friend and one of my spirit guides. He is finally starting to familiarize himself with me. I can't lose his trust now." Sarah returned to her porch swing, perplexed.

How on earth was she supposed to gain this elusive

forest creature's approval? The fox had been a true challenge, and now the bear seemed to be difficult, too. He certainly seemed to have something to say to her. But his fear of humans seemed to overpower his desire to deliver the message.

CHAPTER FIVE

First thing the next evening, as darkness begin to fall over Witchland, Sarah cloaked herself and Addie in an invisibility spell. After a long day of working on some simple local cases, which she did as a continuation of Michael's practice and to earn a modest living, she was ready for some sleuthing. She had been jiggling her legs in anticipation all day. Addie was trembling and running around with excitement as well, relishing the thought of joining her owner on one of their classic adventures.

Though Sarah typically used a spell to camouflage with her surroundings, she was learning new spells and trying them out. This invisibility spell was exciting because it made her completely see-through.

The winds of change I feel are right,

> *The wind is warm, and the sky is bright.*
> *Invisibility, please come to me,*
> *Keep me safe from all that see.*

Yet, Sarah noticed it did not muffle sounds the same way the camouflage spell did. "I think this spell may not be as great. But at least we're trying something new, right, Addie?"

"It's okay. I like it," Addie replied. *"But the silence of the camouflage spell does work better. It completely blends us in with the surroundings."*

Sarah and Addie padded across the town to the tiny, misshapen hut with the crooked stovepipe where Harriet lived. Smoke flowed from the stovepipe now, and an odd odor hung around the air near the front door. Through the tiny front window, Sarah could see Harriet stirring something in a cauldron inside, her crow, Edgar, perched on her shoulder and bobbing up and down as she spoke to him. The two had a relationship much like Sarah and Addie, or Susie and Zeva.

"I wonder what she's brewing. I know she makes some weird potions, and she always cautions us to stay away because it might cause side effects. She's vague about the side effects part. Maybe I should've looked more into what she brews," Sarah mused telepathically.

"It stinks," Addie whined.

Harriet turned to the door and stepped outside to

toss out some wastewater. She paused, looking around, her long, crooked nose trembling as if she were sniffing something. It almost seemed she was looking right at Sarah and Addie for a moment, but then she looked away. Sarah took advantage of the moment to duck through the open door and perch on Harriet's little bed.

Sarah had never been inside Harriet's place. It was a single room, cramped and crowded with witch instruments, such as wands. Cluttered on shelves and every available space were herbs and worms in jars. Hanging from pegs on the wall were Harriet's few musty, moth-eaten cloaks. Her staff with the glowing crystal that she used to light her way while she foraged in the dark woods at night or in the caves under Witchland leaned against the doorframe. Dusty books were stacked haphazardly on the floor and on chairs. One hung from a hook above the cauldron, and it was open to a recipe; the steam from the potion brewing beneath it was wrinkling and warping the pages.

Sarah squinted and managed to make out, "for the trapping of white-spotted bats, take two teaspoons of newt excrement, four teaspoons of dandelion . . ."

She reminds me of the witch in Hansel and Gretel, Sarah thought.

Harriet turned back inside as Edgar began squawking furiously. "I know, I know, hush," Harriet

49

muttered to the bird as she returned to her potion. After giving it one stir with her long-handled spoon, she began to wave her fingers in the green steam rising from the bubbling liquid. She emitted an eerie moan and then began chanting ominously:

Oh me, oh my, I hope to curse Sarah Spellwood tonight!
Make her lose her tongue in an important meeting,
Make her fumble over every greeting.
May she not sleep a wink,
So that Madras may take her in defeat!

"Hey!" Sarah flashed out of her invisibility spell. "What on earth are you doing—?"

"I got you!" Harriet cackled and stooped to slap her thighs. Then she began to guffaw hysterically and fell to the floor, Edgar flying off her shoulder as she began to roll back and forth with the force of her mirth. Edgar landed on the bed frame, where he squawked and bobbed up and down, his eyes glittering with equal hilarity.

"Are you serious?" Sarah snapped. "That was a joke?"

"I so got you!" Harriet howled, red in the face now and pointing at Sarah. "Oh, the look on your face was priceless! Hahaha!"

Sarah scowled and shook her head, waiting for

Harriet to get over her laughter. When Harriet finally managed to stand back up, Sarah started to talk, but Harriet interrupted her by bursting into laughter once again. "Are you finished?" Sarah finally asked.

"I think so—no, I'm not." Harriet laughed for a bit longer.

Addie whined impatiently and sat. Sarah sighed and sat back on the bed. "Well, I'm glad you got a good laugh."

"It was funny." Harriet pulled her enameled newt eye from her pocket and flashed it at Sarah. "Since you took me to get my cataracts removed, I've noticed the funniest thing—this newt eye gives me X-ray vision! I can see right through your silly spell." Harriet cackled.

"That's great, Harriet," Sarah said exasperatedly.

"It is. It's hilarious." She giggled, stuffing the eye back in her pocket.

"I am investigating you," Sarah explained, feeling embarrassed that she had been caught. Harriet was always good at embarrassing her.

"Oh?" Harriet smirked. "For being too sexy?" She winked at Sarah before chortling, Edgar joining in.

Addie flattened her ears. *"This is serious!"* she admonished them both.

"For the murder of Arnold Packington," Sarah went on. "I found your energetic traces near the treasure he buried in the woods. I believe you found it."

Harriet laughed. "That old thing? Of course, I found it. No one knows the woods like I do."

"Okay, but Malorie was the one who dug it up. So did you just take a few things from it, or what?" Sarah asked.

"What do I need gold and rubies for?" Harriet snorted. "I have everything I need right here."

Sarah paused, then decided to believe her. Harriet was the only person she could think of who would plausibly find a priceless treasure in the woods and then not take anything from it. "So you found it and didn't touch it?"

"Oh, I touched it. Opened it up, looked at it. Edgar likes shiny things." Harriet shrugged. "Then I shut it and covered it up again. Arnie sure thought he was clever burying it there, but I found it right away."

"You found it right after it was buried?" Sarah asked.

Harriet nodded. "The day after, from the looks of it."

"When was this?" Sarah inquired.

"Oh, I don't have any concept of time. Sometime in the '90s, I think, maybe the '80s. When that Clooney guy was president."

"Clinton," Sarah corrected. She frowned. "Okay, so why did I sense Madras near there? Can you tell me that?"

"I'm sure Madras wanted to get her paws on it. She didn't, though," Harriet said. "Probably never found it. That ghost doesn't know the woods as well as I do."

"Okay. One last question. Did you see who might have killed Arnie? Do you know anything about that case?"

Harriet shook her head. "I'm not the sleuth here, Miss Spellwood."

Sarah sighed. "Well, thanks, Harriet."

"Sure thing! Next time, it might be easier to knock." Harriet winked and then began to chuckle. "Though I kind of enjoyed pranking you. That look on your face!"

Sarah, feeling flustered, thanked Harriet and began to leave with Addie trailing behind her. As she stepped out of the little hut, Harriet called after her, "I need a ride to my eye appointment soon!"

"Great," Sarah muttered. "I'll be here, but you need to let me know when," she told Harriet.

"I'll just show up at your house under an invisibility spell and surprise ya." Harriet winked, and Sarah could still hear her laughter through the door after she shut it.

CHAPTER SIX

"I THINK WE HAVE A GENUINE MYSTERY," SARAH said excitedly. She sat in Eli's passenger seat as he drove them to Buffalo, New York, to meet his mother and stepfather. His cautious driving and the new car scent that somehow remained in his car, despite the fact he had had it for over a year, made Sarah love him all the more. How could one man be so perfect? Neat, clean, organized, kind, *and* handsome to boot!

But Eli's jaw was tense. Sarah placed a hand on the back of his neck and asked, "You look a little stressed out. What's up?"

"Well, we're going to my mom's house. I'm the family disappointment, considering she's a lawyer and I just became a cop." He sighed. "She's a hard woman to please."

"How could you be a disappointment? You are so

wonderful! You save Witchland every day." Sarah squeezed his arm comfortingly.

"Thanks, my love." He smiled at her. "She never explicitly states how she feels. But I just sense that she wanted me to take the lawyer path, too."

Sarah felt a tiny knot of nervousness form in her stomach. "Well, hopefully I will be good enough for her. How was she with your other girlfriends? And your ex-wife?"

"Honestly?" Eli glanced at her, an anxious expression on his face. "She was terrible. She hated my ex-wife."

Sarah groaned. "That's not good."

"But none of my girlfriends or my ex-wife were anything like you," Eli said in a rush. "I think my mom will appreciate how happy you make me, and the fact you're an accomplished real estate attorney. She's very protective of family, so she needs to see I'm happy with someone. Plus, you've got a lot of grit to you. You're definitely someone she would respect, anyway." Eli smiled at her reassuringly and placed a hand on her thigh.

"Let's hope so," Sarah breathed. "I'm trying to distract myself by thinking about this mystery."

"Can you turn the air on? I'm hot," Addie panted from the back seat, where she sat buckled in with a special doggie belt. It was important to her to accom-

pany Sarah buckled in and sitting up like a human. Sarah wouldn't dream of leaving her at home, especially not for such an important event as meeting Eli's mom.

"It's January," Sarah chided Addie. "The air outside is cold."

"I'm dying in here," Addie said dramatically.

Since they didn't often leave Witchland, Sarah had only been in a car with Addie a few times before. She had noticed that Addie tended to become very pushy and dramatic on car rides. Her heart melted. She said softly, "Addie, do you have anxiety right now?"

"No!" Addie swiftly denied. *"I just have thick fur."*

Sarah smiled and rolled down her window a crack. She knew Addie well enough to sense she was lying. Eli winced as the cold air hit his skin, but didn't protest. Sarah was grateful to have found a man who was as compassionate toward animals as she was.

They finally reached Buffalo, just as rush hour started. The packed traffic did not help soothe Sarah's nerves. As they made their way through many twisting streets into a swanky neighborhood, lined by handsome houses and leafless maples that were probably gorgeous in summer, Sarah hunkered down in her seat. *I've defeated horrible men in court and saved Witchland from pure malevolence a total of four times! I can't be afraid of Eli's mom!* she admonished herself.

Eli finally pulled into the driveway of a beautiful brick house with a stained glass window over its massive oak door. It looked as if it had been built at the turn of the twentieth century, but had been lovingly cared for and remodeled over the years. "This is where you grew up?" Sarah asked, taking in every detail of the gorgeous property.

"Most of my life, yes," Eli said. "My mom and I started out in a much smaller apartment downtown before she made partner and her career took off. You won't believe it when you meet her, but my mom was a waitress all through law school, and she was a single mom for most of my childhood. She didn't let her marriage to my dad, or the struggle after he left her, hold her back from her career."

"Strong woman," Sarah remarked with admiration as she stepped out of the car. Her nerves kicked in again as she let Addie out. Addie bounded onto the manicured lawn and ran around in circles, barking excitedly to finally be free of the cramped quarters of the back seat.

Eli reassuringly took Sarah's hand and led her to the front door. He pressed the doorbell button set into an ornate gold plate. Sarah admired the matching gold knocker and checked her hair and teeth in its reflection to make sure she looked presentable.

The door flew open, and Sarah's jaw dropped at

the sight of Eli's mom. Now it was clear where Eli had gotten his looks. There was a distinct resemblance in their strong jawlines, lustrous blond hair, and sky blue eyes. Eli's mother was the sort of woman who only looked better with age, more distinguished and well put together. Her hair was in a perfect bob with icy platinum highlights, and her nails were perfect, too. Her skin was so flawless that she had to be wearing foundation, yet she looked so natural that Sarah wondered if she was even wearing makeup at all.

"Hi, I'm Sarah!" Sarah blurted, kicking herself for the childlike way her voice sounded. *Am I still in high school or what?* she thought.

"Hi, I'm Mrs. Strongheart," Eli's mom replied coolly, appraising Sarah with a tiny, frozen smile on her face.

"Mom," Eli groaned.

"But you may call me Ruth," she added, glancing at her son. Then she grinned and enveloped him in a hug. It was obvious that as stiff and formal as she was, she loved her son dearly.

Sarah nodded awkwardly. "Well, nice to meet you, Ruth."

Addie bounded up to the door and stuck her wet nose on Ruth's leg to take in her scent. Ruth cried out and jumped back. "You brought a dog," she stated, clearly irritated.

"My dog goes everywhere with me," Sarah replied, stung that Ruth did not seem fond of Addie.

"I don't allow pets inside," Ruth replied crisply. "She will have to stay outside. I wish you had informed me of this before." She shot her son a scolding look before turning to go into the house.

Eli sighed and showed Sarah the way to the yard. As he undid the gate, Addie looked at Sarah mournfully and said, *"Why is she treating me like a bad dog? I didn't do anything wrong, did I?"*

"Of course not, Addie." Sarah sighed, patting her dog's head lovingly. "Some people just don't like dogs or dog hair on their furniture. It will be okay. I'll come out and play with you soon." She watched sadly as Addie entered the yard, sniffing the grass to find out information about her new place.

"I wish I could go inside and scope it out. I need to make sure there is no danger awaiting you, Sarah," Addie said woefully, taking her nose from the grass and gazing at Sarah.

"I'll be okay. Eli will protect me," Sarah assured her. Her heart was heavy as she followed Eli into the house, leaving Addie to stare despondently after them.

The interior was immaculate and well decorated. Sarah spotted some gorgeous epoxy resin wood furniture that she recognized from a craftsman in Witchland. Eli saw her surveying it and explained that he bought Ruth an item for Mother's Day every year. Sarah smiled, touched by Eli's love for his mother.

Ruth ushered them into her living room and offered them coffee or tea. She served Sarah her tea while studying her carefully. Then she sat primly across from them on a small settee and asked, "So, Sarah, I hear you are of the legal profession as well."

"I am," Sarah said, setting down her teacup. "I specialize in real estate law, though I have branched out into some environmental law in Witchland."

"Environmental law," Ruth repeated coolly, nodding. "And where did you go to school?"

"Columbia Law," Sarah replied. "I graduated magna cum laude."

If Ruth was impressed, she did not show it. Instead, she changed the subject by pointedly asking, "So, I hear you are a divorcée."

Sarah was startled by the question, but she was also quick on her feet. "Yes, as is Eli," she pointed out.

"Mom," Eli said tersely. "There is no need to bring that up."

"Of course not." Ruth gave her a fake smile. "How rude of me."

"I understand that you want the best for your son," Sarah responded civilly. "You probably want to know why it ended, and if the same might happen with your son, right?"

A slight smirk played on Ruth's lips. "I would like to hear about it, yes."

Eli began to protest, but Sarah shushed him and began to tell the story of how her marriage with Jeff had unraveled. At the conclusion of her story, Ruth sighed, seeming pleased. "Well, I certainly understand a man being threatened by his wife's career. The same happened to me when I actually finished law school. My ex-husband just couldn't handle his wife being an attorney. I suppose when he married me, I was just a lowly waitress, and he assumed law school was a little phase of mine, that I would soon drop out or flunk out to wait on him hand and foot." She laughed. "When I actually graduated, I think he was quaking in his boots! Eli never really knew him."

"I get birthday cards from him from time to time," Eli said. "I usually don't even write back."

Sarah nodded sympathetically and touched his arm to comfort him. He forced a smile and asked, "So when is the boyfriend coming home?"

"Anytime now. He is picking up dinner," Ruth replied. Then she shot Sarah a sly look. "I scarcely have time to cook. Do you cook?"

"Not really, though I try," Sarah admitted.

Ruth's reaction was impossible to read. Sarah felt as if she had made some breakthrough by relating to Ruth on the similarity of their failed marriages, but that progress seemed gone now. Ruth had returned to scrutinizing Sarah, interrogating her as if she were on the witness stand.

"I suppose you are into that witchy mumbo jumbo that all Witchlanders love? Especially being a Spellwood yourself?" Ruth asked.

Sarah was not sure how to proceed. Then she thought, *Don't be ashamed of something you cherish about yourself! Your witchcraft is an integral part of who you are, and you denied it for most of your life.* Straightening her spine, she cleared her throat and announced, "Yes, I am a witch."

Ruth responded with a slight smirk. "Interesting." Before she could say more, the door opened. A middle-aged man entered, and Ruth introduced him as her boyfriend, Lyle.

Lyle reminded Sarah of her own father with his bald spot and glasses and boring clothes. From what Eli had told her, she knew that he, too, was an attorney. He warmly greeted Eli and Sarah before pecking Ruth on the cheek she offered him. He set Boston Market bags on the table, their aroma making Sarah's mouth water.

"Did you remember to get Sarah a vegan option?" Eli spoke up.

Lyle groaned and slapped his forehead. "I forgot! I'm so sorry! There are potatoes? And pasta salad?" he offered helpfully.

"They are probably made with milk and butter, and there is probably meat gravy on the potatoes, so I can't eat them," Sarah said apologetically.

"I sure am sorry." Lyle sighed.

"It's no problem at all. I can run out and get something separate," Sarah replied.

Ruth said, "I never understood such aversion to meat and animal products in your generation."

"It comes from my empathy for anim—" Sarah began to explain.

Ruth cut her off. "I am aware of the vegan agenda, and I don't care to listen to how I should stop eating meat if I love animals. I may not look it, but I come from a line of farmers, and their work was perfectly honorable."

"I never—" Sarah protested, flustered. But Ruth ignored her as she stood and moved into the dining room.

"I'm sorry. Don't let her get to you," Eli told Sarah. "I'm going to say something."

"Don't. I can stick up for myself," Sarah told him.

"Well, let me go find you a vegan meal," he offered.

"I would like to get it, actually, if I can have the keys, please," Sarah told him. She needed some time away to prepare her strategy for surviving the rest of this unpleasant visit. Eli handed her his keys, and then she politely excused herself and left. She took Addie with her.

As she cruised downtown, looking for a restaurant where she could eat, she couldn't help but think about how cold and critical Ruth seemed. *Okay, I can't be weak. She is just a tough opponent in court. This is all an act to try to scare me off or crack me. I am better than that,* Sarah told herself.

"*She doesn't even like animals,*" Addie whined sadly from the back seat.

"I know. She's terrible. But she's Eli's mother, and I have to make a good impression," Sarah replied. "Thank our Goddess she doesn't live too close or visit often."

When she finally found food and returned to the house, she felt stronger in her resolve on how to handle Ruth. She apologized to Addie as she put her back in the yard and returned inside.

"Can we eat?" Ruth demanded when Sarah appeared in the dining room, holding the bag containing her vegan Chinese dish.

"Let's eat," Lyle said cordially.

Dinner was uncomfortable. Ruth and Lyle talked about their Alaskan cruise and their upcoming trip to the Australian outback. Lyle waxed poetic about his hunting conquests and his dream of one day partaking in an African safari. Though Sarah attempted to explain to him how such safaris only harmed the African savanna ecosystem and perpetuated racism, he did not seem receptive. Afterward, they retired to the living room with glasses of Merlot, which Sarah accepted to be polite even though she only liked white wine.

Lyle suddenly directed a question at Sarah. "Any interesting cases come your way lately, Sarah?"

"Well," Sarah said, "I am actually trying to crack an old cold case in Witchland. The murder of Arnold Packington and the disappearance of his treasure."

Lyle raised his eyebrows. "You know, I used to run in the treasure-hunting crowd. They're a real back-stabbing bunch."

Even Ruth looked surprised by this revelation. "You never told me this," she said, seeming annoyed.

"I actually visited Witchland once, long before Eli moved there, before I even met Ruth. I tell you what, you should look into some of the usual suspects in the treasure crowd." Lyle got up, went into the other room, and emerged again with an address book.

"You know who the treasure hunters in Witchland are?" Sarah asked, surprised at this unexpected lead.

"Well, they live all over, but they often meet up in Witchland or Hanover. I'm not sure if all of them are still living, but I can give you their names." Lyle rifled through the address book and rattled off some names and addresses, which Sarah eagerly wrote down.

"Thank you so much. These are promising leads," Sarah cried.

"The police always suspected competitors," Eli agreed. "This would be a good place to start. We probably have some more current information for these guys in Packington's file."

"You don't," Sarah informed him. "That lead was never properly explored."

"Well, isn't that just how these cold cases go? We can't prosecute so many cases where the culprit is obvious because the police absolutely bungle it," Ruth declared. Then she glanced apologetically at Eli. "Of course, that doesn't apply to you, darling. I'm so proud of you, solving that murder case for the Witchland town clerk that you had two years ago so well."

"I couldn't have done it without her help," Eli said, clapping a hand on Sarah's thigh. Sarah smiled at him.

Ruth nodded slowly, her eyes narrowed. "That is quite a serious ethical breach, involving a civilian in your cases. I hope no one finds out and prosecutes you." She took a sip of her wine, still surveying Eli and Sarah for their reactions.

"That isn't an issue in Witchland," Sarah said firmly. "People there look to me for protection and help with their problems, including police matters."

"I see." Ruth nodded. Then she said, "And what about your partner, Eli? Doesn't she help you with police matters?"

"Of course," Eli said.

"What is her name again? Oh, yes, Jenna Mora." Ruth smiled. "I like her. I actually expected you two to start dating."

"Well, we didn't, and I'm with Sarah now," Eli said with finality.

Sarah felt a prickle of hurt that Ruth brought up Jenna, especially since Jenna had formerly had a thing for Eli. But after hearing Eli's defense of her, a swell of happiness replaced the hurt.

"Ah. Well, I have your old bedroom ready," Ruth informed Eli. "I don't think there will be enough room on that little old bed for the both of you," she added. "Sarah is welcome to the guest room."

"Trust me, we'll be fine in that bed. We sleep in a twin at her house, as well," Eli said.

Ruth did not seem pleased to hear this. "Well, whatever you two want to do, I suppose."

"I can't leave Addie outside all night, so can I bring her in?" Sarah asked. "She's a really good dog," she added when Ruth frowned.

Ruth appraised her with the same coolness that she had possessed all night. "I just don't like dog hair over all my furniture, and she looks like she sheds."

"In that case," Eli said, suddenly standing, "we won't be staying here tonight."

Thank you, Sarah thought. Her love for Eli bloomed even more in her heart.

"What are you going to do? Drive back to New Hampshire this late?" Ruth demanded, a shocked expression on her face.

"We will get a hotel that is pet friendly," Sarah said, also rising and walking to the foyer to get her coat.

"You didn't have such a problem with dogs when we had Bingo," Eli added. "I find it funny you only take issue with Sarah's dog. You've been chilly all night toward my girlfriend, and I'm tired of watching it."

Ruth sputtered, staring at them over her wine-glass. Eli curtly said good night to her and Lyle, then led Sarah out to the car. Sarah fetched Addie and slid into the passenger seat. Just as she clicked her belt in, feeling defeated, she realized that she could not leave on this note, letting Eli defend her and never speaking up for herself. "Just a minute," she told Eli, undoing her seat belt and swinging her leg out of the car.

"What are you doing?" Eli asked.

"Your mom may not like me, but I am determined to make her respect me," Sarah replied.

"Sarah, that's a bad idea," Eli called. But Sarah was already striding toward the front door.

Ruth answered when Sarah knocked. "Have you come to apologize?" she asked tartly.

"No," Sarah replied.

Ruth looked taken aback.

"I can see that you don't like me, and I'm sorry about that, because I'm actually a great person when you get to know me. But I will not be disrespected. I love Eli with all of my heart, and I will be around for a long time if Eli will have me. I actually want to take the next step with him. You don't have to like me, but I would appreciate your blessing," Sarah said.

Ruth stared at her for a long moment. Just as Sarah was about to walk away, Ruth finally said, "You may bring the dog in. Just keep her off my white couches." She turned to walk away, then added over her shoulder, "And, Sarah, on the contrary, I do like you. I see the way my son looks at you, and I see the fire in your soul. You have my blessing." The coolness in her face had softened. Clearly Sarah's speech had made a favorable impression upon her.

Sarah and Eli spent the night. In the morning, Ruth took them to breakfast at a restaurant that she had ascertained served vegan food beforehand. For the first time the entire visit, she even smiled genuinely and laughed at a joke Sarah told.

"Did you cast a spell on her?" Eli whispered in Sarah's ear jokingly.

"No, but I earned her respect," Sarah whispered back. "She isn't nearly as scary as Madras, so she was easy to stand up to," she added.

Eli beamed. "I love you," he told her.

After breakfast, they prepared to return to Witchland. Sarah stood awkwardly at Ruth's door, wondering if a hug was in order, when Ruth offered her hand. The handshake was much warmer than it had been the previous day. Ruth smiled and told Sarah to take care of Eli. "I will," Sarah promised, beaming.

On the drive, Sarah reflected on how serendipitous Lyle's information had been. Eli's mother's house was the last place where she had expected to gain insight into her case. The entire thing had gone well, she thought.

"What are you smiling about over there?" Eli asked affectionately.

Sarah squeezed his thigh. "I think everything is going to work out just great."

CHAPTER SEVEN

SARAH LAUNCHED HERSELF BACK INTO THE mystery of Arnie's murder as soon as she and Eli returned to Witchland. She had a civil case to work on, but she knew it could wait until the next day. Diligently, she began to lay out contact information for the old treasure hunters in Arnie's circle. Surveying the list of names and addresses, Sarah muttered, "I know one of you is a traitor, and I will find you."

"*Which one seems like the culprit to you?*" Addie asked. She lay at Sarah's feet, content after the trip. Being allowed to go inside Ruth's house and sleep at the foot of Eli's childhood bed had delighted her. All of the new scents and experiences had been enough to completely tucker her out by the time they got back to the cottage.

"I'm not sure. I can't tell just by looking at their

names. But I will know when I interview them," Sarah responded. She had a strange leaden feeling in her gut as she surveyed the names, as if at least one of the names was of a vindictive person. "I don't like the way these names make me feel. There is definitely something valid here."

Just then, her phone rang. It was Eli. "Hey, babe," she answered.

"Malorie is missing," Eli said.

Sarah's blood ran cold. Her grip tightened on the phone. "Malorie? I just hiked with her three days ago."

"It happened yesterday while we were in Buffalo," Eli said.

"Who made the report?" Sarah questioned.

"She had some guests at her bed and breakfast, and they became concerned when she never showed up to serve them dinner yesterday. They looked around for her and inquired at the shops to see if anyone saw her. They waited all night, but she never turned up. Jenna just told me that Susie came in and filed a missing person's report," he explained.

Panic gripped Sarah's chest. Not only was Malorie an important business owner and one of the town's three elected mayors, but she had also become Sarah's friend. Most people in the town did not know about Malorie's secret identity as a shapeshifting fox, but they knew there was something odd about her and accepted it. Her place in the town had become so valuable that everyone regarded her with affection and respect. Sarah couldn't shake the feeling that something terrible had happened.

"I think this might have to do with Arnie's case," Sarah muttered. "Malorie had his treasure, and all of the wealth from selling the gold and jewels, so someone must have abducted her to punish her or try to get the money back. I suspect Madras might have something to do with this, or the culprit behind Arnie's murder." The last option made Sarah feel sick. "If it was Arnie's killer, then I sure hope Malorie is okay."

"I hope so, too. We better act fast. Do you have any hunches about where we can start searching?" Eli asked.

"Let me contact Oscar Reedy. He can help us track her." She said goodbye to Eli and hurriedly called up Oscar.

"Well, hello to my favorite attorney," Oscar answered in his hearty voice. Formerly, Oscar ran a hunting lodge and guide service in the Mount Katribus woods, but with Sarah's help, he had given up hunting and simply operated a guest lodge now. He was always ready to help Sarah, whenever she needed him.

Sarah quickly summarized all that had happened.

"I'm on it," Oscar assured her. "Meet me at the lodge in fifteen. Let's track Malorie."

Sarah hurried to the lodge, Addie loping behind her. They greeted Oscar, who had donned his camo and carried a loaded rifle.

"I don't think we need a gun," Sarah said, eyeing the weapon with discomfort.

"You never know," Oscar said.

"I prefer to work things out peacefully instead of with violence," Sarah insisted.

Oscar reluctantly put the rifle in the back of his Range Rover. "You better hope that we won't need it," he said edgily as he began to follow Sarah down to the base of the trails.

"We won't," Sarah promised him. "Remember how I scared off that poacher, Lester, with just magic? I can do that again."

Oscar laughed. "That's one of my favorite memories. All right, let's find this fox lady." He put on his glasses and turned to Addie. "Do you smell her anywhere?" he asked.

Addie began to meticulously sniff the forest floor and brambles overhanging the path. Oscar cautiously followed her, turning over leaves with a walking stick and surveying various animal and human prints in the mud. After a few moments, Addie cried, *"Here! I smell her!"* She let out a woof, and Oscar hurried to her side.

"Sure enough, looks like Malorie was here," he commented, turning over a leaf and picking up a small piece of red hair. "Judging by the footprints, she was in fox form."

"That's weird. She almost never shifts into fox form. She feels it's too dangerous," Sarah mused with growing distress.

"Probably smart thinking," Oscar agreed.

Oscar and Addie continued up the mountain, following Malorie's trail. Suddenly, directly in front of the spot where Malorie had found Arnie's buried treasure, the trail went cold.

"What makes me nervous is that I've seen a few of the same human footprints, made about the same time as Malorie's fox footprints, following her trail. Makes me think someone was either following her or walking along with her," Oscar explained, scratching his balding head.

"I can't see Malorie leading anyone up here but me," Sarah muttered. "Unless someone forced her along."

"And see this?" Oscar pointed to a strange scrape in the mud. "Something was being drug here. I think it was a rope or . . . a dog leash. Looks about the same age as these prints, too."

"Someone was leading Malorie by a leash!" Sarah exclaimed. "Well, I'm going to try to read this trail's energetic imprints on the forest," she added. "Maybe I can see who this was. Thanks for all of your help."

"No problem." Oscar watched Sarah for a moment, fascinated by her magic, as she closed her eyes and tried to focus on the energetic trails left by Malorie and her captor. Sarah found she couldn't focus with his eyes boring into her back.

"Excuse me, but can you not watch me, please?" she requested.

Oscar looked disappointed but agreed and walked down the trail to a place where he could no longer watch. Sarah immediately felt guilty, but she needed her space to work.

Closing her eyes again, she dredged up the energetic trail. There were countless trails made by butterflies, squirrels, foxes, wolves, and other animals. There were also a few trails from people. She located the trail that was left behind after she and Malorie had visited the buried treasure's former site a few days before. Using that feeling, she was able to look through the other trails and find a much stronger, more recent one that matched Malorie's aura. With great concentration, she allowed the energy to envelope her, using her extreme empathy to channel Malorie's emotional state.

Fear. Intense fear. But also rebellion and anger. Malorie was not one to tolerate being led by a leash without a fight. She was furious with her captor, and eager to escape him. Yes, him. There was a masculine energy, a dark energy . . . one that reminded Sarah of someone, though she could not place who.

Madras?

Sarah snapped back to the present. Addie whined, "*It's her, isn't it?*"

"Yes, I think so," Sarah said, knowing that Addie was referring to Sarah's vicious ancestor.

"*How could she be here?*"

"It's not her exactly, but someone working for her, someone who was able to infiltrate the defenses we have against Madras in these woods. I feel . . . well, I sense it is someone I know, but I can't place who. It's the weirdest feeling, like when you have a word on the tip of your tongue but you just can't say it," Sarah said. She grappled with the feeling, trying her hardest to identify who it was.

"*Can you tell what happened to Malorie?*" Addie inquired.

"Well, what'd you find?" Oscar called from up the trail.

"I felt her, and then she was gone. I think she was transported somewhere magically." Sarah groaned and shook her head. "This is not good, not good at all."

"I should've brought that gun, huh?" Oscar called.

"No need for a gun," Sarah called back to him. She then joined him and explained what she thought had happened. "I'm going to speak to the Leekins and

Lativia," she informed him. "Can you see if you picked up anything on your game cams?"

"Gee, I'll try, but my game cameras aren't anywhere near this area or the old trail," Oscar told her. "But I'll go look now." He headed away, and Sarah and Addie headed toward the ghostly clearing to find Lativia.

As Sarah entered the ghostly clearing, the hairs on her arms stood on end. The clearing slowly dimmed, and then she could see the ghosts enjoying their eternal party. There was Michael, holding a goblet of ghostly blue wine and chatting with another ghost. He smiled when he saw her. "Sarah!"

"Michael!" Sarah happily hugged him, not minding that her arms always passed right through him with an electric jolt.

Michael bent down to pet Addie, who wagged her tail eagerly.

"You haven't been leaving the clearing much lately," Sarah commented.

It had occurred to her the other night that Michael had not been visiting her as often. She really hoped that it didn't mean that he was starting to get ready to cross over to the beyond place where all ghosts eventually went when they had no more business with the living. While she knew he deserved to cross over and rest eternally, she also hated the thought of their conversations truly ending now. It would be like losing him twice, just as she had lost her aunt Beth twice, once when Aunt Beth died, and then again when she crossed over two years ago.

Michael merely smiled at her and said, "That's because I can tell you can handle things on your own. I'm old and tired, Sarah." He said the last part in a joking tone, but it only deepened Sarah's fears.

"Well, I'm not sure about that now. I really need to speak to Lativia," Sarah told him. She turned to face the spot where Lativia's throne usually sat and put all of her energy into summoning her witchy ancestor.

Soon, Lativia and her throne materialized. Lativia looked as gorgeous as ever, but her appearance was faded, like a reflection in glass. While most ghosts looked like that, Lativia had not until recently. Sarah's fears of losing Lativia and her assistance, as well, filled her. Lativia made it no secret that she was eager to cross over as soon as she felt Sarah was ready to be entirely on her own. *When will that be?* Sarah wondered anxiously.

"Sarah Spellwood," Lativia said ceremoniously. "You are here about your fox friend?"

"Yes! Have you seen her?" Sarah cried.

Lativia nodded. "Clover Figcreek and her water crew did. They said she was being led by a scary man.

Some city slicker that they have never met before. He smelled like rubber and car exhaust."

"Rubber and car exhaust," Sarah repeated, puzzled about what clues that scent may offer.

"I smelled that but didn't know what it was from!" Addie chimed in.

"That man is working for Madras, I sense," Sarah said grimly.

Lativia sighed. "That is what I feared, as well. I had hoped that my sister was gone from these woods forever, but she is forever discovering ways to get in."

"How could she know that Malorie would be a good target?" Sarah asked, feeling exhausted by Madras's endless attempts to get into Witchland and work her devilish magic. "She must know something about the treasure and Arnie, but how?"

Lativia lapsed into thought for a moment. Then she said, "My sister still possesses a powerful scrying mirror, whose twin I own. I shattered mine and gave pieces to people and Leekins that I must keep in contact with. Clover Figcreek has one; you have another."

"I have a shard of your scrying mirror?" Sarah asked, taken aback.

"Think of the things you took from your aunt Beth's house to remember her by," Lativia hinted.

Sarah realized that one of her mementos of Aunt

Beth's included a small compact mirror that she kept buried in her things in a trunk under her bed. She had not looked at the compact mirror for years. "Is that it?" she asked.

Lativia nodded, sensing Sarah's thoughts. "That is how I have watched you over the years, seeing if you were ready to accept your true destiny and take over my job as defender of the forest and of this town."

"That explains so much," Sarah said. Then she sighed. "Why didn't you tell me about this before?" The tiny crumbs of information Lativia occasionally fed her never seemed to be enough. There was no end to the new things Sarah found out. She often wondered if it would just be easier for her ancestor to sit her down and tell her everything in an hour or two.

"I didn't suspect my sister could also access that mirror, but it appears she has found a way. That would explain how she knows what you are thinking. Knowing my sister, she probably wanted that treasure for herself, and probably even questioned whoever murdered Arnold Packington in an effort to discover where it was buried," Lativia went on.

"I thought as much," Sarah said, shaking her head. "I hate how her greed hurts so many people."

Addie whined sympathetically, and Michael nodded gravely. As a victim of greed himself, Arnie's death clearly upset him deeply.

"She has probably enchanted someone to take Malorie and somehow get the treasure," Sarah concluded after a few moments of mulling over what Lativia had told her. "But that makes no sense, given the fact that Malorie has already sold the treasure and turned it into capital for her businesses."

Michael's eyes grew wider as he realized what Sarah was saying. "Of course, Sarah! Malorie turned the treasure into capital for her profitable businesses and multiplied the fortune. Madras wants to get a hold of that money to make up for missing out on the treasure."

"So she wants to somehow possess or coerce Malorie into becoming one of her pawns so that she can live vicariously through her," Sarah cried. She understood how Madras worked now, living through demons and other people that she used as her minions. "Well, she won't have an easy time breaking Malorie down, but we still need to save her."

CHAPTER EIGHT

As Sarah returned home from the woods where she had been speaking with Lativia, all she could think about was getting a shower in, getting into her comfortable sweats, and relaxing with some iced tea on her porch. She was startled out of her thoughts when Addie let out a warning bark and bounded ahead. "What is it, girl?" Sarah asked.

"I can smell someone at the door!" Addie cried.

Sarah rounded a corner and could see her porch clearly. Then her blood ran cold. Addie kept running toward the very familiar figure standing at her door, his forefinger pressing on her doorbell.

"Oh, no. Things just got really bad." Sarah called to Addie. "C'mere, girl, stay by me."

"What can I do for you?" Sarah asked brusquely,

removing her key from her pocket as she strode past her ex-husband, Jeff, and began to unlock her door.

"Sarah," Jeff said unceremoniously. "I—I didn't know if you were home or not."

"I am now." Her door jiggled open, and she pushed inside. Addie stopped for a moment to suspiciously sniff Jeff's pant leg before trailing after Sarah.

Sarah turned to face Jeff, reeling at how familiar his face was yet how he seemed like a perfect stranger, someone she had known in another lifetime perhaps. She had never seen him look so disheveled and unkempt. His eyes were bloodshot, and his breathing was slightly ragged, as if he had run all the way from Chicago. He was also badly in need of a shave. However, his pressed suit and strong cologne were still the same as the last time she had seen him across the table in the mediation room for their divorce.

He was smiling warmly, as if he had not just walked out on her in the midst of their tenth year of marriage without a word of explanation or apology. "Can I come inside?" he urged after an awkward moment, seeming perplexed at the defensive way Sarah stood in her doorway.

"No. I just want to know what you want. The divorce was finalized long ago," she replied. "There shouldn't be any more affairs to settle."

"I just wanted to check on you, you know.

Everyone at your work—your old work—they told me you went crazy and disappeared after your boss let you go. It took some digging to find you, since you don't have social media anymore and you changed your name back." He glanced at the nameplate on her door and frowned. "I didn't think you would ever change your name back. You hated the notoriety of it so much."

"Well, I'm not a Lawrence anymore," Sarah replied tartly.

Jeff shifted from foot to foot awkwardly. "Well, it was your business listing that led me to you finally. Glad to find out you're okay."

"I'm fine." Sarah paused, totally unable to comprehend how to handle this moment. In the past, she might have snapped something like, "What do you care?" but she found that she no longer wanted to lash out at Jeff. Having Eli in her life and knowing her spirit animal team, a fabulous familiar, and her true identity as a witch enabled her to let go of most of that pain. While some still lingered, she no longer nursed it, hating Jeff and wishing he would never find happiness. She simply wanted peace and harmony, for herself and for him.

"Well . . ." Jeff shifted uncertainly. "I'm staying at the bed and breakfast in town. It's a nice little place, though the owner is a bit weird."

"That's my friend, Malorie," Sarah retorted. "She's also one of the town's mayors." She narrowed her eyes, realizing that Jeff must have seen Malorie recently. Her gaze trailed down to the ground. And also . . . he was wearing brand-new Wellington boots! The new rubber smell! Sarah gripped the doorjamb.

"One of the mayors?" Jeff smirked. "This is an odd place you chose, Sarah. I'm guessing this is Michael Howler's office? I recall he had moved here. Where is he living now?" He appraised the little cottage with his steely gray eyes. Everything about his posture was condescending and critical.

Sarah remembered her piercing green eyes used to make Jeff crumble, so she looked him in the eye. He glanced away uncomfortably.

"He passed on," Sarah finally said, folding her arms across her chest, recalling many awkward dinners with both Jeff and Michael. She had not seen it back then, but now she realized that Michael simply did not like Jeff and had made it as plain as he could without betraying his manners. How had she missed so many signs, like Jeff's pompous derision of everything that was dear to her, or his condescending attitude that hung around him like a bad odor?

"I'm sorry!" Jeff looked genuinely surprised. "Tell me—did you just take over his business?"

"He left it to me. And no, it's not an asset I owe to you," Sarah responded.

Jeff scoffed. "My, you have a really defensive attitude now. I'm not here for money or assets, Sarah."

"Then why are you here?" Sarah began to pet Addie's head to calm her anxiety. Her heart was racing.

"I don't like him," Addie told her telepathically. *"He smells like rubber and car exhaust, too."*

"That's because he came from Chicago and he's got new boots. I think he's our man. That's why the energy felt so familiar to me!" Sarah replied telepathically.

"What should we do?" Addie asked with a thrill in her voice.

"Nothing for now. Let's see if Jeff trips himself up or gives us a clue," Sarah replied. *"We have to act natural, the way he would expect us to act."*

"I just wanted to catch up. For old time's sake." Jeff shrugged. "If you're not interested, I understand, but it's been a long time. I thought we could talk. Just like old times. Meet me for dinner tomorrow at the little Italian place—what's it called?"

"Geno's," Sarah replied. "And sorry, but my boyfriend, Eli Strongheart, would not appreciate that."

Jeff looked taken aback. "Eli Strongheart, huh? Is he some kind of Witchland warlock or something with a last name like that?" His tone was mocking, as was the little smirk that played on his lips.

"He's actually the town police chief," Sarah responded curtly. "And he's sure interested in what happened to Malorie."

"Something happened to Malorie?" Jeff's reaction appeared genuine, but Sarah had already learned that her ex-husband was a hard man to read. She had not even guessed he resented her successful career after ten years of living with him!

"Yes, she disappeared today." Sarah noticed the corners of his mouth twitched.

"That's horrible. Maybe I should find a new place to stay. Anyway, it's just dinner, to catch up. I'm sure your boyfriend won't mind," Jeff said.

Sarah was suspicious that he changed the subject so fast. As she started to object, Addie interjected, "*Sarah, this would be a great way to pump him for information.*"

Sarah forced a fake smile. "I suppose he wouldn't mind. It would be nice to catch up."

Jeff smiled like the cat that got the canary. It made Sarah feel nauseated.

"See you at five tomorrow, then? I'm sure they're closed now," he said crisply.

"Sounds good." Sarah then shut the door. Through the little window at the top of the door, she observed Jeff staring for a second, looking perplexed. Then he shrugged and turned away.

Sarah exclaimed loudly, "I sure didn't expect to see him! I don't want to have dinner with him at all. I don't need Jeff in my life anymore!" She sat down on her rocking chair, needing to collect herself.

Addie wagged her tail. *"You never did. You've always been so strong."*

"I've done a lot of growing and healing since coming here. You know, the one thing I always did during our divorce proceedings was beg Jeff to tell me why he had left. He would never tell me why; he would just look at me like I was so pathetic. It really hurt my soul! I used to fantasize about seeing him again and asking him one final time, making him tell me. Yet I finally saw him, and did you know that I didn't even think to ask?" Sarah grinned as Addie rested her head on her lap. "I guess I really have moved on. I don't even think about him anymore, at all."

"That is so great," Addie agreed. *"But I think he's our guy. He's the one who abducted Malorie."*

"It's just like Madras to choose him. She probably thinks he's my weakness. But I'm too strong for that." Sarah suddenly recalled the conversation about the mirror in her possession. "Hang on," she told Addie, hurrying up the stairs to retrieve the little compact mirror. "I need to close this little spy portal before Madras spies on me again!"

With Addie on her heels, she went to Daisy's

apothecary. To her surprise, Daisy was reading animal oracle cards with Frida. It always surprised her to see the two witches acting like friends, despite their long rivalry and frequent bickering. They were, in many ways, similar, but also polar opposites. *Just perfect for a best friendship*, Sarah mused.

"I have a problem," Sarah announced after the witches greeted her warmly and listened to a brief rundown of her Buffalo trip. She laid the compact mirror on Daisy's counter. "This is a shard of Lativia's ancient scrying mirror, shaped into a compact. I think Madras is spying on me through it. You know that big mirror I found in her cave chamber? I think she is watching me through that."

Daisy surveyed the mirror, frowning. "Mirrors are quite powerful instruments in magic."

Frida also picked up the mirror. "I don't get a bad feeling from it," she said.

"That's because it is simply a window into the between world, a world where you can find portals or doors into other worlds. Mirrors are often used for spying, seeing the future, or connecting with the dead. That is because they are technically open pathways to that between place, and once you access that place, you can find portals into whatever world you want if you know how," Daisy explained.

"Well, I know that," Frida said, rolling her eyes.

Sarah sighed. "So is there a way to close the portal? I don't want to destroy this mirror. It was my aunt Beth's."

"I do remember her using it," Daisy said fondly, thinking back to her long friendship with Sarah's aunt. "Don't destroy it! You know who is good at these sorts of things?"

"Who?" Sarah inquired.

"Harriet," both Daisy and Frida said at once.

Sarah groaned. "So she will mercilessly tease me and then maybe do it for me—but maybe not." Dealing with Harriet was always a hassle to Sarah, though she had developed a great fondness for the quirky witch as well.

Thanking Daisy and Frida, Sarah went to Harriet's crooked hut at the edge of the village. Harriet was outside, feeding breadcrumbs to Edgar and singing to him in a raucous, screechy voice. Sarah cringed, but Edgar seemed to love it, judging by the way he was dancing and flapping his wings on Harriet's wrist.

"Spellwood," Harriet said, without even turning.

"Harriet," Sarah responded.

Harriet turned to face her, grinning. "My, my, look at you today, dressed down and on a mission. You came to bother me because . . . ?"

Sarah held out the compact mirror and explained what she needed Harriet to do.

Harriet held the mirror and grinned. "Well, this is easy enough. I just have to blacken the mirror out."

"Don't do that," Sarah rushed to say. "It's precious to me."

"I'm not going to black it out on this side, silly. I will put a spell on it so that anyone who tries to watch you through it only sees blackness. I can also set a spell so that they can't listen. I can set a noise they can hear instead—maybe some music. Let me guess, you like the Backstreet Boys? 'Bye, Bye, Bye'?"

"I do not love the Backstreet Boys," Sarah said.

"You sure? I can see you being a fangirl, in the front row, screaming for Justin to look at you," Harriet teased.

"Justin Timberlake was in NSYNC, not the Backstreet Boys, and 'Bye Bye Bye' is also an NSYNC song," Sarah explained. Then she immediately regretted it as Harriet burst into cackles.

"Well, of course! You're an NSYNC girl. You know all the words. Sure, we can do NSYNC." Harriet giggled.

Sarah rolled her eyes. "Whatever works. Maybe that song will be so annoying that Madras won't even try to channel me anymore."

"See? Win, win." Harriet then shut her eyes and clasped the compact between her palms. She began to mutter with growing volume.

Black, black, be all spying eyes can see.
Black as night, black as a crow's feather,
Cloud spying eyes like bad weather,
And where sounds should there be,
"Bye Bye Bye" by NSYNC shall play,
All night and all day.

She opened her eyes and cracked a grin. "Should be all finished now."

Sarah accepted the mirror back from Harriet. "Well, thanks. That was easy enough. Can I test it now?"

"What, you don't trust me?" Harriet appeared offended.

"I do—"

Harriet cackled. "I'm just teasing you. Find a mirror, any mirror, and ask it to show you your mirror. Imagine seeing your mirror with all of your being. What you see should prove it works."

Sarah nodded and thanked Harriet. Edgar bobbed his head at her, and she thanked him, too.

"That was odd," Addie said.

"It always is with that woman. But I'm glad she's doing well," Sarah admitted.

At her house, she did what Harriet had instructed in her bathroom mirror. At first, nothing happened. But when she concentrated harder on seeing herself through the compact, the mirror began to cloud, as if from shower steam. Then it instantly turned jet black and "Bye Bye Bye" began to blare as if from concert speakers, making Sarah start and Addie bark.

Sarah suddenly started giggling. "Okay, I have to admit, that's pretty funny. Let's see how Madras likes that." Feeling grateful to Harriet, Sarah told the mirror she was finished and it cleared, becoming a view of her bathroom again. Thinking back to what Daisy had said about every mirror being a tool for scrying, Sarah realized that this mirror may as well be a two-way one for witches. She repeated Harriet's spell on it and the other mirror in her bedroom. Content that she was now safe from spying, she poured herself some iced tea and settled on her couch to relax.

CHAPTER NINE

Eli showed up to spend the night shortly after Sarah settled on her couch. He was freshly shaved and showered. Sarah propelled herself into his arms while Addie jumped around, frantically barking for joy. After Sarah stood on her toes to kiss him and revel in the delicious smell of his aftershave, she dropped back down to her heels and frowned.

"What's wrong? I can tell something is up," Eli chided.

"Well, before you hear it from someone else, my ex-husband came by earlier. I haven't seen him in years, and he just showed up on my doorstep," she explained. "I am sure he's working for Madras and that he abducted Malorie."

Eli's mouth fell open. "Was that the city slicker I saw walking down the street? Tall with dark hair?"

Sarah nodded. "That's him."

"Was he bothering you? Threatening you?" Eli frowned. Sarah knew that he would do anything to stand up for her.

Eli's protectiveness always made Sarah feel warm and fuzzy inside. She snuggled into his chest, squeezing him close, as she told him about the bizarre encounter.

"If he just wanted to say hello like a typical ex, then he would have simply called. It's definitely weird he showed up here in person," Eli surmised. "And smelling like the guy who took Malorie, too."

"I wasn't happy to see him, that's for sure." Sarah sighed. "That's why I hate the idea of having dinner with him."

Eli looked uncomfortable. "I have to admit, I don't like the idea of you going to dinner with him at all."

"I assure you, Eli, there's nothing there," Sarah swore.

"I know that. But he's probably dangerous. What if he's here to abduct you, too?" Eli asked.

"I doubt he's that stupid. And, actually, I have a plan. I may not even have to go to dinner with him. I'm going undercover in an effort to catch him talking with Madras or something," Sarah said.

Eli still looked unhappy. "This worries me, Sarah."

Sarah kissed him reassuringly. "You know that I

can take care of myself. But I really do appreciate you worrying about me."

"Of course. I love you," he replied.

"I love you, too. And, besides, I will do anything to get out of dinner with that man," Sarah said.

Eli then made a teasing face. "Okay, so you still think I'm better-looking than him?"

"Stop." Sarah laughed, playfully punching his arm. His muscles always impressed her. Though she didn't want to say it and seem immature, she secretly agreed that Eli was much more her type than her ex-husband. Seeing Jeff and thinking of their crumbled dreams had not hurt her at all. That wound had closed.

Briefly, Sarah recalled their dreamy plans to go to Paris and feed each other chocolates at romantic sidewalk cafés and stay somewhere with a clear view of the Eiffel Tower. Those plans had gradually disintegrated under the weight of their busy work schedules and then their eventual divorce. Now, Sarah enjoyed Witchland and her life with Eli so much that she had not yearned for the romance of Paris at all. That seemed like another life now.

She regained her serious composure as she began to prepare for a night of spying on Jeff under an invisibility spell. Eli uneasily went to bed, still uncertain about her plan. "I really wish you could relax," he told her. "You've had a pretty long day."

"I know, but my friend is in danger. I have to save her," Sarah replied. She placed a kiss on Eli's head, then turned to Addie. "Find Kelvin and follow me, in case I need you two to intervene." With a quick bark, Addie raced away.

Under the spell that helped her camouflage with her surroundings, Sarah strode to Malorie's bed and breakfast. There were two guest rooms upstairs. It was not difficult to figure out which was Jeff's, as she could hear his voice on the phone through the door.

Pressing her ear against the door, she heard him saying, "She agreed to dinner with me, so I don't know what else you want me to do. I have to play it slowly. Sarah is not dumb."

After a pause, he added, "You underestimate her—yes—well, yes. I will take care of her. Okay, I will do it tomorrow . . . Tonight? But she's sleep—oh. Yes, I understand. I will get it done tonight." Then, after another pause, he said, "Yes, the prisoner is well. I just checked on her and fed her. Yes, I think the enchantment is working . . . Well, her eyes are dark, for one thing."

Sarah's heart began hammering in her chest. *Where is she?* she wondered frantically.

Jeff stopped talking. Sarah realized that he must have hung up the phone. He began moving on the other side of the door, and Sarah had to jump back while maintaining her concentration on her camouflage spell as he let himself out.

In the dim light of the hallway, Jeff truly looked crazed. His eyes had a strange, haunted light, and his mouth hung open at an unnatural angle. With shaky steps, he descended the stairs two at a time. He definitely appeared worse than when Sarah had seen him earlier.

Sarah followed him onto the street. Her alarm increased as she realized he was heading to her own house. *Is he planning to kill me or something?* she thought with horror.

Reaching the house, Jeff paused, chewing one of his nails. He had never had that habit when Sarah had been married to him. With strange jerky movements, as if he were controlled by marionette strings, Jeff circled the house. Seeing all of the windows dark, he began to try to climb up the trellis that led to Sarah's bedroom window. The flimsy wood snapped under his foot, and he crashed onto the grass.

Sarah had to suppress a smirk as her bedroom light flicked on. Eli rapidly appeared on the porch, his gun drawn. "Show yourself!" he bellowed.

"Sorry," Jeff stuttered, struggling up from the ground. "Uh, is Sarah home?"

"What do you want, creep?" Eli bellowed again. "Let me guess, you're Jeff?"

"Yes, and I'm here to take care of you," Jeff replied sinisterly. He raised his hands and began to chant a spell in a guttural voice that was not his at all. His eyes began to glow green, a sickly Madras green.

"No!" Sarah screamed. She broke out of her spell and crashed toward her ex-husband. Just as she was about to tackle him, Addie and Kelvin emerged from the woods, Addie in her wolf form. They charged him.

With a scream, Jeff flailed as the wolves tore at his clothes. Sarah seized his arms, and Eli ran over and handcuffed him. "You, Jeff Lawrence, are under arrest for attempted breaking and entering. I'll see what else I can throw at you, too, when we get to the police station," Eli declared.

Jeff began to recite another spell. Quickly, Sarah hit him with a blocking spell. He was enveloped in white light and reeled back from the force of Sarah's magic. For a second, he rocked on his feet, looking dazed. Then he shook his head as the white light faded and glanced around, clearly confused. When he finally looked at Sarah, he started back, bumping into Eli. Eli hefted him back up by his handcuffs.

"Sarah? What—what are you doing here? Where am I?" Jeff demanded.

"Nice try," Eli growled.

"No, Eli, I really think he has no idea where he is.

Madras got a hold of him somehow and enchanted him. He wasn't himself," Sarah told her boyfriend.

Jeff gaped at her. "What—what is going on? Why am I in handcuffs?"

"You need to go back to Chicago, Jeff," Sarah said firmly.

"I never even left Chicago," he sputtered.

"You're in Witchland. I won't explain how, but you need to be careful back in Chicago. Have you met anyone strange lately, someone new, probably a female?" Sarah asked.

Jeff blinked at her. "Well, that's a funny way to ask if I am seeing anyone. Yes, I just started dating someone special, for your information." He looked around again, still lost.

"She is not who you think she is. She only means you harm. Now you need to leave," Sarah said.

"I—don't even know what happened," Jeff pleaded, starting to cry. This experience had clearly broken him. "And why are there wolves?" he added, seeing Kelvin and Addie still circling him, their fangs bared.

"Ask him where Malorie is," Eli suggested.

"Where is Malorie, Jeff?" Sarah pressed.

"Who is Malorie?" Jeff cried.

"I figured he doesn't remember anything. He was under a spell this whole time. We're just going to have to find her some other way," Sarah said.

"I know where she is," a loud, deep, booming voice filled Sarah's head.

"Nope, I'm outta here!" Kelvin cried. *"I don't like bears!"* He put his tail between his legs and started to run off.

"Kelvin, stay, we need your help!" Addie pleaded.

Kelvin hesitated on the edge of the woods, staring into the dark trees opposite him. Sarah also stared as the lumbering dark shape of a bear stepped out of the shadows toward them.

"Whoa! Whoa!" Jeff screamed.

"Stop it," Eli demanded. Reluctantly, he began to unlock Jeff's handcuffs. "Now get out of here and don't come back," he ordered, turning to face the approaching bear.

Jeff took one last frantic look at Sarah before running off into the village, toward the bed and breakfast.

"Hello, bear," Sarah said, walking toward the bear cautiously.

"My name is Scar," the bear answered, sitting back on his haunches to survey Sarah. Sarah then noticed the wide, thick scar emblazoned across his throat and chest. He was a monstrous black bear, very fat from recently emerging from hibernation and eating everything in sight to gain the weight that he lost during the winter. A few dead leaves from last fall

clung to his fur. His eyes glistened with intelligence and emotion.

Addie let out an instinctive growl. Though she was very discerning of who was actually friend or foe, her innate canine distrust of bears was not easily dismissed.

"Hi, Scar. I'm Sarah Spellwood," she replied.

"*I know. I have been watching you for a while,*" the bear replied.

Sarah smiled, thinking of the shadow she had once spotted in the woods.

"*I am here to offer you my help,*" Scar said, "*but I also need your help in return.*"

"You know where Malorie is? Can you take me to her?" Sarah asked, her heart beating faster. She already had a sense that this bear was her new spirit animal, and she cherished him already. There was something intensely comforting about his presence.

"*I know where Malorie is, and I will take you to her. But she's not in immediate danger. I need urgent help for my family first,*" Scar told her. "*They are the ones in immediate danger; I fear they may not make it through the night.*"

"Eli, I have to go help these bears," Sarah told her boyfriend, Scar's sense of urgency overtaking her.

Eli's eyes widened with worry. "Really? Sarah, tonight has already been so dangerous. What if Madras enchants Jeff again and he comes after you? Or what if something else equally horrible happens in the woods?"

"I don't think anything like that can happen, since Madras isn't allowed into the village or the woods, so she can't get to Jeff. I'm more worried about him returning to his sweetheart in Chicago," Sarah assured him. Then she smiled. "But you're welcome to tag along, so that you can help out if needed."

CHAPTER TEN

As Sarah followed Scar through the woods, she realized her eyes could not penetrate the gloom. She decided to shapeshift into a wolf. Eli looked disconcerted, as he always did when he saw Sarah change, but he did not waver in his resolve to follow her. With him, Addie, and Kelvin flanking her sides, Sarah felt completely safe. Then she heard a fourth wolf. She looked over to see Michael's ghost, shapeshifted into a huge gray wolf and padding alongside her. Sarah grinned, relieved that her entire pack was here to help her save Malorie, defeat Madras, and save the bears who were in trouble.

They soon came upon a cave built into rocks and trees. Inside was a large black bear, huddled protectively over her cubs. Sarah had not realized a mother bear was settled so close to the town, but there she was.

Her cubs had just been born as she left hibernation; they were usually born in late January or early February. Though black bears were rare near Witchland, their numbers had been increasing with the recent revitalization of the forest. Through her thick, musky scent, Sarah could also smell warmth, kindness, and mother's milk. Sarah began to feel nervous, for she had never spoken to a mother bear before. She was not sure how a mother bear might react to the presence of four large wolves, either.

She heard a buzzing sound and turned to see two Leekins, who looked like blurs as they hovered on their wings. They landed on a rock in front of the den. Sarah recognized Clover Figcreek and Mathan, the caretaker of bears within the woods. They greeted her and then flew into the den first. Clover Figcreek began to light up, much like a firefly, casting the great mother bear in gentle blue light. That was when Sarah noticed the two mewling bear cubs cuddled into their mother's belly. The bear gazed mistrustfully at the pack of wolves that had just trotted up to her den.

"They're not real wolves, just spirit ones; they come as friends," Clover Figcreek promptly told the bear.

"I found them. They can help us," Scar assured her.

The mother bear relaxed slightly. *"Well, I trust what you say, Clover Figcreek. Your people helped my sick cubs."* She turned to face the wolves again, while glancing briefly at Eli. *"Who are you all?"*

Sarah decided to morph into her human form. She wanted the bear to fully trust her. "I'm Sarah Spellwood, ancestor of Lativia Spellwood," she introduced herself.

The bear nodded sternly. *"I have heard of you. Your name is known far and wide as a champion among animals."* The bear then turned to see Michael change from a wolf to his ghostly human form, and she softened even more. *"Of course, Michael Howler, I know you, too. You are dearly missed among our kind."*

Michael bowed his head at the high honor of the bear's recognition.

"And you." The bear surveyed Addie as she shed her wolf form to take on her golden-collie mix appearance. *"You are that one I see running around with that troublemaker wolf."*

Addie widened her eyes innocently. *"Troublemaker? He doesn't mean any harm."*

"We just don't care for wolves," the bear replied, her voice gruff. *"Or their dog descendants."*

"What is your name?" Sarah asked gently. She placed a protective hand on Addie's head. Addie wagged her tail submissively, trying to get on the bear's good side.

The bear seemed interested in keeping the peace,

nevertheless. *"Miwak,"* she replied. She began to push a small pile of raw, pungent fish toward the trio. *"You are welcome to eat the fish I caught today."*

"I just ate," Sarah lied out of politeness, recoiling from the smell.

"It would go right through me," Michael joked, pointing to his translucent, glowing ghostly stomach.

Addie eagerly ran up to the fish and began to wolf it down. Miwak seemed pleased that someone wanted to share her dinner. *"Delicious!"* Addie cried, licking her chops. Miwak preened herself.

"What is wrong?" Sarah asked. "Scar said you needed our help."

Miwak seemed stricken with grief. *"Well, Scar is my mate. Our cubs aren't well, and I fear we are losing them."* She gazed down at her cubs with deep sadness in her eyes.

"Can I look at them?" Sarah asked.

Miwak reticently reared up to sit on her haunches, revealing her cubs fully. Being a black bear, she was much smaller than a grizzly, but her size and stature still awed Sarah. The cubs mewled and rolled on the ground, trying to soak up their mother's body heat left behind on the earth.

Sarah gasped. "They are the cutest things I've ever seen!" Eli also let out a gasp at their tiny faces and round ears. But upon closer inspection, it was obvious that they were not well. They were soaked in sweat and shaking.

Miwak begrudgingly nodded for Sarah to approach the cubs. Sarah began to rub their fur, tantalized by how soft and cuddly they were. They felt warm, but not feverish, and they did not appear to be in any pain.

Michael commented, "It is so good to see bears start to populate these woods again. There used to be many here years ago, but hunting drove them out. Your kind was not here when I was still walking these woods alive. There are only four thousand black bears total in New Hampshire as it is. Your cubs are certainly a blessing."

"I am not the first bear to come here," Miwak explained. "There are a few you didn't even know about. But Scar and I are not from here; we came from Canada. We heard this forest was a safe place, so we made the long journey. I knew I had cubs inside my womb, and I wanted to make sure they would not be shot. We were always in danger in my homeland, always being clubbed to death in our hibernation dens, hunted in our forests, shot for eating people's unwanted garbage, killed just for our hides, fur, and fat." Miwak covered her face with her meaty paws. Sarah got the sense that she was thinking of family and friends she had personally lost. "Here, we are safer because of the magic in these woods, but the *journey was hard on us. We owe our health to the Leekins."*

"We also want to keep you safe," Sarah assured her, feeling Miwak's distress like sharp pricks in her heart. She had never previously considered the plight of the bears, but it bothered her. Now she knew she had to get involved. "We are trying to expand our woods, too, and make all of this mountain a protected forest, so that there is no hunting at all. Then you and your cubs would have hundreds of acres to roam, undisturbed."

Miwak looked pleased with the idea. Her eyes shone as she imagined a safe haven for her cubs to grow up in.. But then she became somber again. *"I do not want to lose my cubs, especially with many more cold months ahead of us."*

"I will get the town vet. He is a kind man, and he will save your cubs," Sarah said. She turned to Eli and asked if he could radio for Jenna to fetch Clifford Artemis, the town vet. Eli quickly did that, and a few minutes later, Jenna radioed back that Dr. Artemis was on his way. Eli ran down to meet him at the base of the woods and lead him to the bear den.

Sarah, Michael, Addie, Kelvin, and the Leekins waited with the bears until they heard leaves crunching under heavy boots and saw the beam of a flashlight cut through the woods. They ushered Dr. Artemis over.

As he began to survey the cubs, Scar said, *"Thank you."* There was a soulful gratitude in his voice.

"You are very welcome. I hope they recover quickly," Sarah said. "Dr. Artemis is a wonderful vet, and he will take care of your cubs."

"Thank you, as well," Miwak said. *"You may count us as your spirit animals, as well."*

"We will always guide and protect you," Scar swore.

Sarah smiled and bowed her head, humbled by the honor. Saving animals always made her heart swell with happiness. "Okay, can you please take me to Malorie? I need to save my friend before it's too late."

"She is alive, but she is being possessed by something very dark, very foul," Scar told her, leading her and the rest of her friends away from the den. *"Something that makes me shudder."*

"Madras's dark magic," Sarah concluded.

"I have never felt anything like it, and it scares me. But I want to protect your friend and repay your kindness toward my family," Scar went on.

"That reminds me," Sarah interjected, turning to Addie and Kelvin. "I heard you two are being troublemakers," Sarah admonished them. "I have to say, I'm very disappointed in both of you—especially you, Addie. You know better!"

Addie stared up at Sarah, wagging her tail. *"I really*

didn't do anything wrong." She glanced at Kelvin. "We're not troublemakers, are we?"

Kelvin appraised Sarah with his yellow eyes. Then he looked away, guilt written all over his face.

"Kelvin, what have you done?" Sarah asked sternly.

"I was just bored," he admitted sheepishly. "I thought it would be funny to growl at that bear."

"Why would you do that?" Sarah sighed. "She is a mother."

Kelvin looked even more guilty. "I'm a wolf. We don't like bears. Bears or wild cats. We're natural enemies."

"That doesn't mean you should taunt them," Sarah said. "I want you to be respectful of that bear. She's a new mom, and she doesn't need any more threats in her life." Sarah turned to Addie. "I hope you're not joining him, are you?"

"No," Addie swore. "I promise, Sarah. I just like to chase rabbits and squirrels with him, and pee on things to let everybody know we were there. That's all we do. I didn't even know about that bear."

Sarah sighed. "I suppose you couldn't help that." She knew not to foist her human sentiments onto other creatures and impede the natural course of life, but she also felt committed to helping Miwak and her family. She never made a promise lightly.

Shortly thereafter, Addie and Kelvin took off, on the hot trail of a rabbit. Michael shook his head and said, "They'll be back if you need them. They won't go far."

"I know," Sarah said, trusting her canine familiar fully.

Scar led them off of the trail and through a patch of particularly dark, tangled woods. Eli held branches back from Sarah's face as she ducked under them; Michael simply flowed through them. "Looks like Jeff has already been on this path," Eli commented, indicating the vague signs of a makeshift trail through the wilderness with his flashlight.

"So we know we're in the right place," Sarah agreed.

Suddenly, the bear stopped and rocked back on his haunches. *"Here we are,"* he said.

Sarah looked around, confused, for there was no sign of Malorie. Then she realized that the bear was indicating the burrow ahead of them. She beckoned for Eli to shine his flashlight into it, and then she saw that the burrow disguised a much deeper crevice in the rocks, which was hidden under a curtain of tangled roots and moss and old leaves. The curtain prevented Eli's light from illuminating the interior of the crevice any further.

"Oh, that looks creepy," Sarah said.

"The energy here is thick, and bad," Scar said. *"But Malorie is in there. I can smell her fear."*

"I can sense it," Sarah agreed. "She must have been transported here telekinetically by Jeff using Madras's magic. That's why we couldn't trace her here. She is very well hidden. In fact, I'm scared to go in there," she admitted.

"I will give you bravery and the thick skin you need to defeat that evil," Scar said ceremoniously.

He then leaned toward Sarah, twigs snapping under his heavy legs as he transferred his weight forward. She tried not to flinch from instinct as he touched a paw to her forehead. Though she loved all animals, and wanted the bear's power, it still awed her to be so near a wild animal with his scar emblazoned across his chest. Clearly, he was capable of great might . . . and great violence, if needed. Intimidated, she shut her eyes and tried to relax, to give herself over to the bear.

A gentle flow of energy began to creep into her bloodstream, gradually flooding her entire body. It felt like warm honey, flowing mellifluously, bringing with it a gentle tingle that she found quite soothing. Then she felt her chest begin to expand with love and her spirit strengthen with raw physical might. Suddenly, her fear of the crevice did not matter anymore. She was brave, like a mighty bear, ready to overcome even the most formidable of enemies.

She opened her eyes. "I am able to shapeshift into a bear now," she told him. The knowledge that she could do this simply existed within her, much like her knowledge of her ability to change into a wolf.

Scar nodded. *"I have given you this gift. Use it wisely,"* he said. Sarah admired the deep yet soothing rumble of his voice.

"Of course, I never abuse my powers. That is one of my vows, which I will make when I am finally fully initiated as a Wolf Coven sister," Sarah assured him. Then she hesitated.

"What is it?" the bear rumbled.

"I'm worried I might turn to wood while I'm afraid. It's a Spellwood thing. Can that happen when I'm in bear form?" Sarah inquired.

Scar peered at her for a moment. Then he shook his head. *"I don't think so, as I have never turned to wood. But that's an odd ability."* He dropped to all fours. *"What is the plan?"*

"I'm going to enter that burrow and save my friend," Sarah said simply. "Is she in there alone?"

"It seems like it," Scar said.

"Let me go first," Eli begged.

Sarah reluctantly allowed Eli to go ahead. She

followed him gingerly, ready to turn to a bear should any danger rear its head.

Eli swept the curtain of roots back, and some dirt rained down. Sarah slipped in after them. The crevice was a fairly deep surface cave, entirely made of dirt and rock, with barely enough room for the two of them in single file. At the very back, in a pool of shadows that Eli's flashlight dissipated, huddled Malorie. She was in her fox form and looked gaunt. When she lethargically raised her head to look at her visitors, Sarah started. Malorie's eyes looked like two deep, soulless black pools. She was bound in glowing blue energetic chains that kept her unable to move. A dog bowl with some water in it was within reach of her snout, but it was nearly full, giving the impression she hadn't had a drink for some time.

Beyond Malorie was a small pool that had formed in the rock floor. Its black water had a dull, ominous green glow. When Eli shined his light on it, Sarah realized the water was gradually rotating. "Oh, so that's enchanted water. It must be full of the magic working on Malorie. It is probably an effort to zombify her, so that Madras may control her and thus possess her."

Eli shook his head. "Can we just . . . take her?"

Sarah frowned. "I have no idea." She knelt before her friend. "Malorie? Can you hear me?"

Malorie stared at her dully, without a hint of recognition. But Sarah could still feel Malorie's life force; it was not completely replaced by Madras's pure malevolence and greed.

"Chains be gone," Sarah muttered. The chains suddenly grew dark and slithered off of Malorie like snakes before hissing into nothingness. Malorie continued to lie there, not seeming to understand that she had been liberated.

"Eli, let's scoop her up and carry her out of here. I think the magic emanating from the pool is why she's still not responding to us," Sarah said.

Eli gingerly slid his hands under Malorie's tiny fox body and lifted her up. She made a weak mewling sound, like a kitten in need of milk. He turned toward the entrance to the burrow and began to exit.

Just then, the water in the pool started to rotate with more force. Water lapped over the stone lips of the pool, making a hissing sound, as if it were boiling. Sure enough, hot steam began to rise from the surface as the water bubbled menacingly. Sarah shrank away from the pool as a bubble popped and showered her with stinging hot droplets.

"Sarah! Let's get out of here!" Eli shouted. He ran back to seize Sarah's arm and drag her out of the crevice.

"Not so fast!" an eerie voice flooded the space.

The steam over the pool started to converge into the shape of Madras.

Sarah shouted a spell, and it engulfed the apparition in white light, but still the apparition remained. It began to solidify, and suddenly Madras herself stepped forward out of the steam clouds, lowering herself to the ground. The seething pool instantly began to calm.

"What are you doing here, Madras?" Sarah snapped.

"That treasure is mine! It's always been mine! And yet it's still beyond my clutches. Do you really think I would just let it go so easily?" Madras cackled. "That fox is mine! She will make me rich."

"You're a fool," Sarah responded. "Why do you keep coming back? That treasure is not yours. And your sense of entitlement over it makes me even more determined that you shall never get it!"

Madras simply smiled. "Maybe you have defeated me before, but I keep getting stronger and stronger. Getting your ex-husband to work for me was a nice touch, wasn't it?"

"It didn't rattle me as much as you thought it would," Sarah snapped back.

"Perhaps I underestimated how much you have moved on, or maybe Jeff was just an unworthy pawn. All the same, I have a deal for you, Sarah. It's quite a nice one, so I suggest you listen," Madras proposed.

"Go on," Sarah said, narrowing her eyes.

"Give me the fox and let me get rich. And then I won't bother you or this forest again. You can live out the rest of your days in peace, never battling me again, and I will be content with my riches. Really, Sarah, I'm making a huge compromise here. I'm taking only a sliver of this town's riches for myself now, instead of controlling the whole town. We both know that I should be the ruler of the entire town, but I'm willing to settle for less. I have grown, you see? I'm the bigger person. It's really a wonderful deal."

Eli scoffed. "That still won't be enough for you. You'll go on to take more, and more, and more."

Madras appraised Eli coolly.

"Eli's right, and you really don't know me if you think I would just sacrifice my friend so you can get wealthy," Sarah seethed.

Just then, Malorie stirred, making a feeble sound. Then her eyes opened. She cringed back at the sight of the sinister witch in front of her. *"Sarah, be careful,"* she croaked before going limp again in Eli's arms.

"See what you've done to her? Haven't you already hurt enough people over this treasure?" Sarah cried.

"I just want what's mine, and you can't even respect that. What a shameful way to treat one of your elders. If you would only listen to me, you could learn so much," Madras went on.

"What I want to know is how you're even in these woods. We have banned you; we have closed your portal. What did you have Jeff do to get you back in here?" Sarah exclaimed.

Madras merely laughed. "Wouldn't you like to know? He hid the object I used to get back into these woods very well. See, that's the sort of thing you would learn if you simply sided with me."

"Just give that up already. I'm not ever siding with you. I need you to leave my friends and my town alone," Sarah replied.

Madras looked enraged. "*Your* town, huh? You think I didn't grow up in these woods, in a little house even smaller than yours? You think I didn't toil alongside my family, cutting trees for buildings, trying to make a living from the hard soil, hauling water and rocks, and slowly building Witchland from the very ground up? This town is here because of me! You have some nerve coming here centuries later and claiming that it's *yours* more than mine."

"It doesn't matter who built this town," Sarah shot back. "Your goal is to destroy it, to exploit it for your greed. You don't deserve to call this your town anymore."

Madras recoiled, her teeth bared in an ugly grimace of rage. Then she suddenly lashed out with a spell.

"Sarah, watch out!" Eli cried.

But the energy had already hit Sarah. She watched with fascination as it bounced off her skin. Already, her clothes were turning into thick, dark hair, and her nails were erupting into massive bear claws. As she transformed into a bear, she became immune to Madras's magic.

"You need to take Malorie and run!" Sarah shouted. Though she was in bear form, she was able to communicate with Eli with great effort.

"I can't leave you!" Eli cried back.

Michael dashed into the crevice, in his wolf form. Addie and Kelvin tried to follow him into the space, but there was no room.

Eli still refused to leave. He gazed at Sarah with terror in his eyes, not moving.

"I like the little song you used to black out your mirrors. But I still stayed ten steps ahead of you, girly," Madras cackled communicating telepathically to Sarah.

"I just want to know how you're here," Sarah insisted. "The Leekins banished you from these woods and sealed off your portal!"

"I suspect there's some enchanted object in here that is in the pool," Michael said telepathically. "Probably something Jeff brought in."

"Wouldn't you like to know?" Madras snarled.

"I can dive for it since the hot water won't hurt me, but I won't be able to grab the object, whatever it is. It'll pass right through my hands," Michael offered.

"Sure, see if there's something in there," Sarah said.

Madras wheeled on Michael, sending out a flash of dark magic. Sarah was already prepared and stepped in the way, blocking Michael's body from the onslaught of wicked darkness with her tough bear hide. Michael dove into the pool and found it was so shallow that he was not even completely submerged. He raised his dripping wolf head over the steaming surface and telepathically called, "There's an amulet in here!"

"Don't you touch my amulet," Madras snarled.

"Let me guess, it was some gift you had your pawn give Jeff," Sarah said. "Now we're going to get it and destroy it."

"No!" Madras shrieked.

Sarah began to chant a spell telepathically to pull the amulet from the depths of the pool. Energy left her giant bear chest like a tractor beam, causing the amulet to slowly rise from the water. It was a beautiful gold brooch, set with a flashing amethyst. The amethyst was dark and cracked, however. Sarah knew that crystals often became clouded or cracked when exposed to malignant magic.

Madras chanted a different spell to counteract Sarah's. Her own beam of dark light enveloped the crystal. It hovered in the air over the water as Michael clambered out of the pool and shook the water out of his glowing fur. Steam bathed it, but Sarah could still see it, pulsing in the light of the pool. She shut her eyes and doubled her effort. The amulet nudged a few inches toward her. Madras also doubled her efforts, and the amulet moved toward her instead.

Michael snarled loudly.

Madras was momentarily distracted, and the amulet almost flew all the way to Sarah. But then Madras cried, "Freeze, amulet!" and it hovered still in the air once again.

Putting all of her might into her spell, Sarah began to chant one that would shatter the amulet. It began to vibrate with the surge of energy her spell put into it.

"No! Stay together!" Madras chanted her own spell, and the amulet inched toward her.

Sarah repeated her spell. The amulet almost reached her.

Realizing that she could not fight Sarah's magic, Madras suddenly split into dozens of wispy, shadowy figures. They jogged around, cackling. One pinched Sarah on her side, pulling her thick bear fur; another punched her in the ribs. Sarah felt herself start to turn to wood as her bear form flickered, threatening to fade away as she became her human self but cast entirely in wood.

I can't become wood now, she thought, shutting her eyes and willing the bear's form to once again fill her being and take over her body. The wooden feeling dissipated, replaced by sheer might and bravery. She realized that she had become even bigger, covered in rich fur and deep muscle. Her head hit the ceiling of the rocky crevice.

Realizing that she could no longer scare Sarah with her fractured appearance, Madras became one being again. It was disconcerting, watching the shadows all blend together to become one frightening, haggard entity. Madras's eyes glowed a wicked green as she opened her mouth. Eerie shrieking emerged, hinting at the many demons that now made up Madras's spirit.

Madras then started to chant a different spell with a few of her voices, while others continued to chant spells to capture the amulet again. Sarah felt chills all over her body. The presence of such intensely hostile magic made her want to run far, far away, but she stayed rooted to the spot, infused with bravery from her bear form. Suddenly, with horror, she realized that the second spell Madras was chanting with a few of her voices was one intended to poison all of the water in Witchland.

The amulet could not withstand the two antithetical forms of magic being exerted on it and burst into a thousand tiny pieces that rained down on the stone floor. Sarah cringed as one of the shards grazed her snout.

With a bitter cry, Madras said, "Good luck! Your magic may be stronger than mine, but I have just poisoned all of Witchland's water. None of you can keep me out once you're all dead!" Then she disappeared with a pop.

CHAPTER ELEVEN

Sarah rapidly returned to human form. "Oh, my Goddess," she shrieked. She bounded out of the crevice and gazed around the forest. Though it was dark and she could barely see, she sensed something was wrong, as despair rose from all of the plants and trees. In an ilex bush near her, she realized that the small, waxy green leaves were starting to yellow and shrivel, and the holly berries were starting to turn dark. "We have to stop this before everything is dead!"

"This is bad, very bad!" Addie barked.

"I'm going to get Lativia to help!" Michael said, then vanished. Kelvin bounded off into the woods to warn his wolf brethren not to drink the water.

Sarah heard the cries of the Leekins rise up, shrilling through the entire forest. They were immediately aware of the devastation Madras had just caused due to their sensitivity and closeness with nature. With rapid-fire energy, they shot through the forest, looking like balls of light instead of faeries with their speed. Sarah heard them all chanting spells in their high-pitched, insect-like voices as they attempted to clear the poison from the water supply.

"Take Malorie to Daisy's and save her!" Sarah cried to Eli.

Eli took off running, Malorie's limp form in his arms.

Sarah and Addie pelted back to the village behind him. They propelled themselves into Margaret and Hua's house, which they left unlocked. "Guys! You have to ring the village alarms! The water has been poisoned!" Sarah cried.

Both women bolted out of bed. Hua seized her keys to the city hall and ran to sound the alarms. Margaret followed Sarah to her house to grab the spellbook and then followed her and Addie into the woods. She created a ball of magical light between her palms and used it to illuminate the pages as Sarah frantically searched for a spell to save the water. She soon located one and began to chant the words, putting all of her energy into it. But she was already exhausted from her battle with Madras and felt only a weak pulse flowing into her magic.

Margaret began to chant with her, and Sarah felt

more strength flow into the spell. Addie also joined in. Soon, Hua found them and added her energy. It was not long before all of the witches of Witchland filled the woods, walking along and chanting the spell. Even Harriet appeared, chanting in her rickety voice while Edgar squawked from her shoulder. Only Daisy did not join because she was busy tending to Malorie. Soon, their combined magic became palpable waves of light, rippling through the trees and settling into the ground. Sarah could tell when Lativia and the other ghosts joined in because the waves of light went from white to gold and became even stronger.

Leekins swarmed among the plants in masses, nursing them back to health. Sarah stumbled upon a dying squirrel as two Leekins hovered over it, sending light energy into its limp body. Soon, it sprang up and bounded off into the trees, healthy again. Eli soon returned and stayed with Sarah as she worked, even though he had no magical powers to lend to the effort.

As the first wan gray light of dawn filled the frosty air, Sarah had to sit down. Her entire body throbbed with exhaustion. Margaret laid a comforting hand on her shoulder. "The state water inspector just came down and said there is nothing wrong with the water. They're saying it was a false alarm. We did it. And nothing died."

Sarah breathed a sigh of relief. "I'm so tired."

"You should go rest," Eli urged. There were also bags under his eyes as he placed a loving hand on Sarah's shoulder.

"No, no, I have to go check on Malorie," Sarah responded. She struggled up and leaned on Margaret and Hua for support as they helped her to Daisy's apothecary. Eli followed, looking concerned.

Malorie was lying in front of Daisy's woodstove while Daisy knelt over her. The room was strongly scented with the sage that Daisy had burned to exorcise Madras's influence from Malorie. Sarah collapsed into a chair, Addie curled up at her feet, and Eli laid down on Daisy's cot. Margaret and Hua returned to their house once they were sure all was well.

"You're up, Malorie," Daisy cried cheerfully.

Sarah opened her eyes and looked over at Malorie. Sure enough, the fox's eyes were open. Malorie smiled gently at Sarah and then Daisy as she morphed into her preferred form, a young woman with flaming red hair. Sarah noticed Eli was gone and realized that he probably had to go to work on almost no sleep. She admired him so much.

"I can't believe you saved me. I was starting to

think there was no hope," Malorie said, her voice still weak and sluggish.

"*We're glad you're okay!*" Addie barked.

Sarah gathered herself up from the chair where she had fallen into a deep sleep from exhaustion while watching over Malorie. She eagerly hugged her friend, grateful to feel that she was now vivacious and warm again.

"I was so worried about you," Sarah cried. "Your friendship is so important to me. I was afraid I was going to lose you."

"She was sucking the life force out of me. I didn't even know who I was anymore. I just heard whispering voices in my head, and what they were saying scared me." Malorie shuddered.

"Those were the demons that control Madras," Daisy explained. "But we kicked them out of here, and out of you."

"Oh, thank you!" Malorie told Daisy warmly. "I can't believe I was abducted by one of my own clients!"

"Who happened to be my ex-husband," Sarah commented dryly. "Small wonder we divorced, right?"

Malorie stared at Sarah in shock. "He's wicked?"

"No, he is not at heart. He was just enchanted by Madras. Which reminds me, I need to make sure he's left your bed and breakfast. Do you want to go with me? I'll call Eli, and we'll make sure he's gone."

Malorie, normally so spunky and fearless, now seemed to shrink as she nodded her head. "I will be fine, but just for now, I wouldn't mind an escort."

Sarah thanked Daisy and hugged her, breathing in the lovely scent of herbs practically woven into her dreadlocks. Daisy smiled at her warmly. "Don't forget to take care of yourself, Sarah. You did a lot of magic on very little food or sleep."

Just then, Sarah's stomach rumbled audibly. "Indeed, I definitely need to eat."

"Let me whip something up for you at home," Malorie offered. "I was going to make beef wellington the day I was abducted. Oh, right, you don't eat meat. Well, I have rolls?"

"Don't you worry about cooking today," Sarah assured her. "Let's go make sure affairs are straight at your place."

Sarah sent Eli a quick text asking him to meet them at the bed and breakfast. Then they made their way across town. Though she looked well, Malorie moved along at a slow shuffle. Sarah knew it would take some time for her to fully recover. People poured out of shops and businesses to hug Malorie and ask her what had happened. Malorie made up a lie on the spot that she had been abducted by a client in a robbery gone wrong and had been saved by Eli and Sarah. Everyone thanked and congratulated Sarah, calling her the town's heroine.

Sarah smiled and told everyone that they really needed to let Malorie get her rest. She guided her friend to the beautiful Victorian house where she ran her business. Eli met them on the steps.

"I just did a sweep of the house. Looks like that couple you were hosting left early," Eli said.

"Darn it. They were going to stay a whole week! That's nearly a grand I'm losing!" Malorie groaned. "Oh, well, I can't imagine they would want to stay somewhere someone had been abducted."

"What about Jeff?" Sarah asked.

"There's no sign of him in the house, but he hasn't packed his things," Eli said. "That does concern me."

"He might have just fled the town. He was pretty freaked out," Sarah suggested. But she had a strange feeling that she was wrong.

"Well, since I have no guests, do you two want to be my dinner guests tonight? Daisy, too?" Malorie offered feebly.

"How about I cook and we eat together?" Eli offered, winking at Sarah. Sarah grinned, loving the plan.

Malorie agreed. Sarah then led her into her bedroom to lie down. Sarah had never been inside the bedroom and was charmed by how resplendent it was.

Everything was upholstered in rich red velvet, and the massive bed had fake red rose vines twined around its rich mahogany posts. A tiny vanity sat in the corner, bearing gold and pearl jewelry and sparkly makeup that Malorie never wore. Sarah knew that Malorie liked shiny, pretty things, even if she didn't adorn herself in them.

"I'm just so glad you're better," Sarah said, watching her friend fondly as she nestled into her bedding and closed her eyes. She watched Malorie for a moment, ensuring she was all right, before leaving the room and closing the door gently behind her.

"We have to locate Jeff," Eli said urgently. "I don't like the fact he left his things. I don't want to assume he just left."

Sarah shrugged. "I have no clue where he might be if he's still here."

She heard panting and turned to see Addie running up the stairs. *"I just got back from chasing a rabbit with Kelvin!"* she said excitedly.

Sarah sighed. "I don't like you chasing rabbits, remember?"

"Anyway, I saw that hateful man at your house! Jeff!" Addie crowed. *"I barked to warn him to stay away, and then I came to get you."*

Sarah grabbed Eli by his arm and began to run. "Jeff is at my house!"

Jeff was sitting on the porch swing, looking forlorn and bedraggled. But the crazy look of Madras's enchantment was gone from his eyes. As he watched Sarah and Eli approach, he appeared mournful.

"Jeff, what are you still doing here?" Sarah asked. She stopped in front of him, her hands on her hips.

Jeff gazed up at her despondently before sharply looking away, shaking his head. "I, uh, I needed to find out what happened to me. I'm so lost and confused. I feel like I'm going crazy . . . like I was in a fugue state or something. Since I'm here, and you saw me . . . could you tell me what I did?"

Sarah debated telling him the truth or a lie. She hated lying, but she also didn't think everyone was ready for the truth about magic and Witchland yet. Particularly not her practical ex-husband.

"Let's just say that strange things happen in Witchland," she said finally. "You were not yourself, so it's not your fault. Someone took advantage of you, someone very vindictive, and that's how you ended up here."

"Okay, but you said that has to do with my girlfriend back home? I mean, Vickie is great. I can't imagine she would do something, anything, to hurt me," Jeff said.

"She isn't real," Sarah said, her heart breaking at the look that came over Jeff's face. This man had betrayed and hurt her, and yet she did not wish this on him. "She is a figment of Madras, my very malicious ancestor. She used you as a pawn to get to me."

Jeff shook his head, bewildered. "This has to be a hallucination. I can't possibly be here, listening to this, from . . . you."

"But you are," Eli spoke up. "I've dealt with some people suffering psychotic breaks in my days as a cop, especially in Buffalo. I can tell you that you don't usually hallucinate total strangers in as much detail as you're seeing me. This is real, I'm real, and Sarah's real. I apprehended you trying to break into Sarah's house while I was asleep in her bed and she was out."

Jeff groaned. "I can't believe I did that. That's— that's not me, I swear."

"I know," Sarah said gently.

"I mean, what was I going to do?" Jeff stared at her bleakly.

"You were going to do something to get me out of Madras's way so that I couldn't save her prisoner," Sarah replied. "I don't know what exactly, but I imagine it wasn't good." At the look of despair on Jeff's face, she hastily added, "But don't worry, it wasn't you in your right mind. I don't hold it against you."

"I do," Eli muttered. Sarah gave him a scolding glance, though his protectiveness made her feel warm.

"You're too forgiving. If it were me, well, I'd detest

me right now," Jeff said. "Listen, I hate to do this in front of your boyfriend, but I feel I owe you an apology."

"It's all okay. You weren't you," Sarah reiterated.

"No, for before, when I was myself," Jeff pressed on. "The divorce. The way I treated you. Everything. I'm so deeply sorry."

Sarah stepped back slightly in shock. This was an apology she had never expected to receive.

"Well," she finally said. "I have had to forgive you on my own to move forward with my life. I made peace with your actions a long time ago." She turned to Eli, taking his hand. "I've moved on, and I'm so happy."

"That's great." Jeff nodded, seeming sincere but still forlorn. "I hope I can find someone who is . . . real." He then snorted. "I should have known when Vickie wouldn't spend the night. She said she always had work early in the morning. But when I'd call or try to go over to her place, nothing. She only spoke to me when she wanted to. I knew something was up, but I just figured she was married."

"And you still dated her, even though you thought she was married?" Eli snorted.

Jeff fixed his eyes on Eli. "I've been a bad person. For a long time. But that ends now. I have to change my life. I have to change everything." He turned to look at Sarah again. "Thanks for that. That was one thing about you, you always tried to bring out the good in me. I resisted, but now I'm ready."

Sarah bowed her head. "I didn't know I did that, but I am glad."

"Sarah," Eli said, squeezing her hand harder, "you always bring out the best in everybody."

"I have to go now," Jeff said, standing up, his leg shaking slightly from where he had fallen on it the night before. "Thank you," he said a final time, glancing at Sarah and then Eli, and finally down at Addie. Addie stared up at him, wagging her tail. Then he walked away toward the bed and breakfast.

Sarah sensed she would never see him again. But she wished him the best.

She turned to Eli and smiled. "Well. Let's figure out who killed Arnie Packington and then put all of this behind us."

But Eli was bending down onto one knee. "Sarah."

Sarah felt goosebumps erupt all over her skin. "Oh, Eli," she gasped.

"I haven't been entirely honest with you. There was an ulterior motive to Buffalo; I wanted you to meet my parents, but I also wanted their blessing. I also called your parents and got their blessing last weekend."

Sarah felt weak at the knees and overcome as tears of joy started to stream down her cheeks. "Oh, Eli."

Eli popped open the box; the most glorious diamond glinted from the folds of velvet inside. "Sarah Spellwood, will you make me the happiest man on earth and marry me?"

"Yes! Oh, yes!" she sobbed. She threw her arms around Eli's neck and began to cover him in kisses.

Eli had the biggest grin Sarah had ever seen on his face as he stood and slid the ring onto her finger. Sarah's hand trembled as she held it out. She surveyed the ring, turning it around in the afternoon light.

"I love you," Eli said. "More than anything in the world."

"I love you, too," Sarah said softly.

"I honestly had this whole romantic plan to propose to you. Your friends were going to enchant flowers to drop on us from the sky and everything. But this moment . . . well, I thought this moment was perfect."

"It—it was," Sarah agreed.

"You didn't ask me to help," Addie whined.

Though Eli could not hear her, he sensed her disappointment. "You couldn't have kept the secret," he told her, patting her head lovingly.

"That's true," Addie admitted.

"But I was going to have you carry the ring to Sarah. Sorry I didn't do that in the end," Eli added.

"It's okay," Addie said, licking his hand to show him what she was saying.

Then Sarah started to laugh.

"What?" Eli prodded.

"I wanted to ask you to move in with me, but I was too nervous to just come out with it!" Sarah continued to laugh.

Eli grinned. "Of course! I'll move in with you. But we had better get a bigger place."

"I think I know just the place." Sarah winked.

Then, she led him inside by the hand, the weight of her ring on her finger delighting her.

CHAPTER TWELVE

"First on my list to interview is Fred Williamstein," Sarah told Addie as she went through the list Eli's stepfather had given her of Witchland treasure hunters. She checked the town phone book and was pleased to find Fred's number right away. It boggled her mind that the previous Witchland cops had bungled this so badly when tracking down competitors for the treasure was so straightforward. Maybe it was too simple and this was a dead end? Sarah hoped she could finally close this case.

After several rings, Sarah got his voicemail. It sounded like an old-fashioned answering machine, and Sarah pictured tape reeling as she left a brief message asking Fred to call her back regarding the cold case. Then she moved on to the next person on her list, Billy Anders.

Billy was not in the phone book, but a quick Google search revealed that he had moved to Hanover. Sarah obtained the number to his antique shop and called. "Hullo!" a rough voice answered on the second ring.

"Hello, is this Mr. Anders?" Sarah asked.

"Sure is. How can I help you?" The man smacked his gum infuriatingly.

"I'm Sarah Spellwood, an attorney in Witchland," she began.

Billy Anders made a sucking sound, and she imagined him sucking on his front teeth. "I already told Delores, I'll get her the money when I can. Suing me isn't gonna help."

"Well, I'm not sure what you're referring to, but I'm not leading a lawsuit against you. I actually am calling in regards to Arnie Packington."

Billy was silent for a moment. Then he said, "Well, darn, I haven't heard that name in, oh, forty years. Shame what happened to him."

"Yes, it is, and I'm determined to find out exactly *what* happened to him," Sarah replied.

"I see. They never solved it, did they?"

"No, they have not," Sarah said.

"Shame. Well, I wish I could help you . . ."

"You can, actually. I just want to know what your relationship with Arnie was," Sarah replied in her most soothing voice. She knew that if she seemed accusatory or suspicious in any way, Billy could just hang up. She really didn't want to make a trip to Hanover at the moment, but she would if she had to.

"Well, I suppose we were acquaintances. I didn't have anything to do with it, so don't look to me," Billy said defensively.

"I am certainly not accusing you of anything. Clearly the police overlooked something and that's why Arnie's murder has never been solved. People like you, people who knew Arnie, are the biggest chance I've got of bringing justice to him. Please help me bring him that justice; it's been so long. The truth needs to come out," Sarah pleaded in her most persuasive voice.

Billy was silent for another moment. Then he said, "Well, you didn't hear this from me, but he was locked in a dispute with . . . well, you didn't hear this from me, okay?"

"Okay," Sarah pushed, her heart beating faster at the hint of a valuable clue.

"He was in a dispute with Freddy and Merris over that treasure," Billy finished.

"Fred Williamstein?" Now Sarah really wished that Fred had answered the phone.

"Yep."

"And who's Merris?" Sarah inquired.

"Merris Golightly. Just another one of our circle," Billy said.

Sarah nodded, surprised since Merris had not been on Lyle's list. She furiously scribbled down both names and circled them.

"And why do you think they were in a dispute?" Sarah went on.

"Well, they both felt they deserved some stake in it, considering how hard they worked to help him solve the clues and survey old maps. They were going to split it three ways, equal shares. Then he went out and found it all on his own and didn't share a dime. Hid it somewhere and didn't leave any clues for anybody else. Pure selfishness, you know, but that was Arnie. He didn't care about anybody but himself." Billy stopped and cleared his throat. "Like I said, I had nothing to do with it, and I wasn't too awful close to the guy. I am just repeating what I heard."

"Did the dispute ever become violent, to your knowledge?" Sarah asked.

"Not that I know of, but who else would kill him? I bet they held him hostage to get him to crack and accidentally killed him. After all, what good would he be for leading them to the treasure if he's dead?" Billy suggested.

Sarah thought back to Arnie's account of what he could remember about his murder. There had been only one assailant . . . that Arnie had seen, anyway. A male assailant.

"Well, thank you, Billy. Just one last question. Do you know who Stuart Lincoln is? He was the only one who talked to the police about Arnie's treasure," Sarah went on.

"Stu died of a heart attack a few years back," Billy said. "In fact, Freddy may be dead, too. We're all in our seventies and eighties now, dropping like flies."

Sarah grimaced at the depressing statement. "Well, he mentioned treasure hunting. Do you think he knew what happened, or had some part in it?"

"Stu? Naw, he wasn't a violent guy. He wasn't even a treasure hunter. He just liked to buy treasure other people had already found. He was a gem dealer, in fact, and spent a lot of time out West, especially in Tucson, doing the gem shows. That's where he died, in fact. I don't even think he was around when Arnie died," Billy informed her.

"Well, that's very helpful. Thanks for your time, Billy. Please call me if you think of anything else," she concluded.

"Yup, all right." Billy hung up.

Sarah set her phone down and began to search for Merris Golightly. *What a happy name,* Sarah thought as she searched for Merris online. Merris was a bit more elusive, but Sarah managed to track down one of her relatives in California. After a brief conversation with the relative, she obtained Merris's phone number. Evidently, Merris now resided in California in an assisted living facility. Merris didn't answer Sarah's first call, but she called back an hour later.

"Ms. Spellwood," she said graciously. "So good to hear somebody is opening up Arnie's old case."

"Yes, thank you for getting back to me." Sarah wondered why Merris acted relieved to hear Arnie's case was reopened. Was she guilty and trying to pretend that she wasn't? Sarah and Addie exchanged suspicious glances. "I just want to know if you have anything to offer, any new clues."

"Oh, honey." Merris sighed. "I already told the police everything I knew."

"Were you . . . the anonymous tip?" Sarah asked, tapping the police file with the top of her pen.

"I was," Merris said. "I stayed anonymous because, well, everyone thought Fred and I did it. You know, the whole treasure-hunting community is pretty small. We all meet each other at conventions, or run into each other investigating old mines and spots where we think treasure is hidden. People talk, and they all *really* talked about Fred and me. That's why I got out of the treasure-hunting business and just focused on my family and community after that."

"I see. Were you here in Witchland at the time of his death?" Sarah asked.

Merris exhaled slowly. "Yes. And I know that looks bad. But I was there because we traced the treasure back there, to Arnie. He was supposed to split it with us, since we all helped him find the location in Nevada, but sadly, no luck."

"So I imagine you quarreled with Arnie?" Sarah pushed. Merris was looking more and more guilty by the second.

That's when Merris laughed. "Listen, I know how it looks, and that's why the police couldn't know who I was. But I had nothing to do with Arnie's death. And I'll tell you why because at this point, I'm old and have nothing to lose. The treasure was actually a huge cache of plunder that Spanish conquistadors hid in the mountains near Reno. Arnie and I knew Fred wasn't to be trusted, so we found that treasure ourselves and split it two ways. I hid mine in my floorboards and sold it over the years, and put the money into stocks and bonds. Saved a few pieces of gold and jewels and had them made into jewelry for my kids and their kids. I'm a millionaire, and no one knows just how rich I am—that is, until I die and my children read my will. Let's just say they'll be pleasantly surprised." The gloating in her voice was unmistakable.

"Wow, that's impressive. And you didn't fear that

Fred would come after you?" Sarah pressed. She circled Fred's name on her notepad twice.

"Fred never knew. I acted outraged that Arnie had the treasure when Fred came to me about it. I even went with him to Arnie's and staged a big fight. Nothing violent, of course, just lots of yelling and name-calling. Then I told him I was done. I moved all the way across the country and got married. As far as he guessed, I just became a middle-class mom of five." Merris giggled. Then her voice became serious again. "Fred is one of those cutthroat ones. Always out in the woods with a metal detector, trying to find even just a nugget of gold. He scared me. I always felt that if the three of us found the treasure together, he would shoot us in the back and take it all."

"So you think Fred killed Arnie?" Sarah asked.

"I know he did," she replied confidently.

Sarah excitedly thanked Merris for her time and said goodbye. She then turned to Addie. "Funny that Fred hasn't called me back. I think it might be time to pay him a visit. Someone will know where he lives."

"How do you think you'll get him to confess?" Addie asked.

Sarah pondered that for a second. Then she grinned. "I have a plan."

"Ooh, I'm in!" Addie said.

CHAPTER THIRTEEN

FRED WILLIAMSTEIN GLARED AT SARAH OVER THE top of his newspaper when she slid into the booth seat across from him. She had found him at the Witchy Café, where he apparently ate breakfast every day. Sarah normally did not come to the café, since they did not have any vegan options, but she realized that she had spotted Fred once or twice around town before. He had thick, craggy eyebrows and piercing gray eyes that were impossible to read. Something about his gaze gave Sarah the heebie-jeebies. She looked at his scarred hands and got the sense that they were indeed the hands of a murderer.

"Hi, Fred. You haven't returned my calls. I'm Sarah Spellwood," she said pertly.

"I know who you are," he snapped, refusing to

shake the hand she offered him. "I have nothing to say to you."

"*Man, he's surly,*" Addie commented from where she lay protectively at Sarah's feet. "*I don't like him. He smells like utter darkness.*"

"*I don't either,*" Sarah confided in Addie telepathically. But she continued to beam at Fred, trying her best to charm him.

"Every little detail you think of can help me solve Arnie's case," Sarah replied.

"That happened forty years ago. You're not going to solve it now." He snorted.

"Lots of cold cases are solved decades later. I plan to solve Arnie's in the same way," Sarah replied. "I have DNA evidence from blood samples that can crack the case now. That technology didn't exist in the eighties."

"Right. Don't you need someone's DNA in the database to get a match?" he replied.

Sarah smiled. "So I see you know a thing or two about DNA. I imagine you probably keep up with forensic science, don't you?"

Fred glared at her, then decided not to speak. He was aware that Sarah was laying a trap for him.

"Anyway, whoever murdered Arnie did it for nothing, because someone else already got to the treasure. Malorie Vulpes, believe it or not. She found it and has it stashed in her bedroom, right under her bed," Sarah went on.

The rage that flashed in Fred's eyes was unmistakable and deeply disturbing. "Does she now? Well, I hope she enjoys that. That treasure was supposed to be mine, or part of it, anyway." He forced his eyes away from Sarah and took a deep breath, gathering his composure.

"I imagine this is a source of deep pain for you. Especially since the entire treasure-hunting community thought you and Merris had something to do with Arnie's death," Sarah pressed.

Fred suddenly flung his newspaper down and stood up. "I have nothing more to say to you," he thundered. Then he stormed out of the café. The waitress stared at Sarah with questioning eyes.

Sarah paid for Fred's meal and texted Eli, "Fred has left the restaurant."

"I love stakeouts," Eli commented, tearing open a bag of cheddar-flavored popcorn.

"Me, too. It's been a long time. The last time was when that kid kept spray-painting the outside walls of the high school and we had to conduct surveillance all night to catch him." Jenna laughed, biting into a ranch-dipped baby carrot.

Sarah smiled. She was in the back seat behind the partition with Addie and Jenna's boyfriend, Mark, a cop from another town. Eli and Jenna were in the front. They were parked in the police station's SUV in an inconspicuous lot near Malorie's, carefully observing the bed and breakfast. As darkness gathered, they simply had to entertain themselves as they waited for Fred to appear. That was not hard, since they were all friends. Sarah didn't know Mark well, but she liked his laid-back personality and wry sense of humor.

Hours passed. They played kid games, like I Spy, and Sarah read part of a murder mystery novel. It was hard to focus, though, as adrenaline kept pumping through her veins. The vibes she had picked up from Fred had creeped her out to no end. She was excited to capture him.

Around ten, Malorie's lights went off as she went to bed. Sarah wondered if Malorie was afraid. One abduction was enough; the poor fox-turned-woman had been through so much. Fortunately, Malorie had been more than happy to agree to Sarah's plan before Sarah even met with Fred at the café.

Despite her excitement, Sarah's eyes started to get heavy around midnight. Around one, she started awake when Eli whispered, "Do you see that?"

"I didn't even realize I was asleep," Sarah muttered, rubbing her eyes.

Jenna pulled out her night-vision goggles and trained them on the woods behind Malorie's bed and breakfast. "Sure enough, it's him," she announced.

They waited until Fred reached the back door. He was wearing all black, just as Arnie had described his assailant. He furtively glanced around him, then produced a crowbar and used it to jimmy the door open. Immediately, Malorie's burglar alarm went off.

Eli shot out of the SUV as Fred dropped the crowbar and took off into the woods. Eli quickly gained on the old man and dropped him to the forest floor, wrestling him into submission and clapping handcuffs on him. When he pulled Fred's hood back, he declared, "Fred Williamstein, you are under arrest for breaking and entering." Eli then wrestled Fred into a standing position and began to drag him to the SUV.

"You set me up!" Fred bellowed hoarsely when he spotted Sarah standing outside of the SUV.

Sarah simply smiled. "I didn't set you up. Greed just got the best of your judgment."

Malorie came out of the bed and breakfast. She observed Fred as Eli wrestled him into the back of the SUV, which Mark and Sarah had vacated. "Great. You got him."

"Are you okay?" Sarah asked, wrapping her arms around Malorie.

Malorie nodded. "I'm just glad this whole business is over. If you ever find a buried treasure in the woods, don't take it!" She laughed, the sound full of giddy relief.

"*I agree! All of this violence over some metal and stones,*" Addie barked. As a dog, she did not understand why humans did such horrible things for abstract ideas like money. Sarah admired and envied her innocence and wished humans as a whole could be more like dogs, especially her familiar.

After ascertaining that Malorie was stable, Sarah took off into the woods toward the bear den, leaving Addie at the cottage with Kelvin, who had come to see her. Sarah needed to make sure the bear cubs were okay. Dr. Artemis had sent her his bill, which she had gladly paid with an extra donation to help those who can't afford care for their pets. He had mentioned in his notes that the bears had had a viral infection and he had given them some medicine.

Not far from the den, Sarah could smell the bears. Since she had acquired bear powers, her ability to smell them and sense their presence had improved threefold. She made her way up to the shaded entrance of the tiny den where Miwak lived with her little family.

153

"Miwak? Scar?" she called.

"Sarah," Miwak's voice floated into Sarah's mind.

Sarah gently poked her head into the den. In the dim light, she could see Miwak, and there were her two little cubs, nursing. They no longer appeared sweaty and shaky. Sarah gasped at how cute and healthy they were.

Miwak looked at her with moist eyes. *"You saved my cubs, and for that, I am eternally grateful to you."*

"I am so glad we could save them. Dr. Artemis is a good vet," Sarah replied.

"I am so grateful," Miwak said.

Sarah beamed and knelt on the ground. She reached out tentatively and gently laid her hand on one of the cubs. "Oh, they're softer than puppies," she cried happily. With her other hand, she began to pet the other cub.

"Their names are little Miwak and little Scar," Miwak said, pointing to each cub respectively.

Sarah felt her eyes grow as moist as Miwak's. "That is beautiful. I hope your family is happy here. It is a wonderful place for you four to thrive."

"I trust that we will. There is good hunting and delicious fish. It is peaceful. Thank you," Miwak said.

"The only trouble here is Madras, and we always defeat her," Sarah said. "I am sorry about the water-poisoning fiasco."

"Thankfully, I knew the water was bad and did not drink it." Miwak nodded. *"I trust that our powers helped you stop that spiteful and hostile witch?"*

"They did." Sarah smiled. "I am grateful to now possess bear powers."

"You are a special witch," Miwak explained. *"Not many have more than one spirit animal guide. Even your mentor, Michael—bless his soul—only has the wolf as his guide."*

"I am honored," Sarah said.

"Always use your gifts for good. Animals would never pervert their powers for evil. We seek good, balance, harmony," Miwak instructed.

There was a rustling. Sarah glanced over her shoulder to see Scar emerge from the brush. He carried a large fish in his maw. At the sight of Sarah, he dropped the fish and bowed his head honorably. *"The woman we owe our lives to."*

"You don't owe me anything," Sarah said happily. "I am the defender of this forest, and I strive to protect all of you."

"Thank you, again." Scar ceremoniously crossed over to Sarah and placed a loving paw on her head. *"We are honored to call you one of us."*

Sarah cried happy tears as she wished Miwak and Scar luck in their future endeavors. "I am sure we will see each other in the future," she said.

"We will," both bears said at the same time.

Sarah petted the cubs one last time. She felt that this was a gift she would always treasure in her memories. Then she said goodbye to both bears and returned to town.

With the forest saved from Madras yet again and Arnie's murder solved, she felt it was time for her to care for herself. She had not slept well or even had time for a shower in days. Her hair was a frizzy mess as a result. She could not wait to tame her wild mane and get some rest—hopefully in Eli's arms, if he was free. With a smile, she descended the trail to town.

Feeling refreshed from a shower, a meal, and a full night's rest, Sarah solemnly journeyed to Arnie's house with Addie trotting by her side. As soon as she stepped foot on the porch of the dilapidated Victorian, she felt Arnie's presence swarm around her. She sat on the step, and Arnie took shape next to her, also sitting.

"It was Fred," Sarah said.

Arnie didn't say anything.

"I think you knew it was him, too," Sarah said.

Arnie still didn't reply.

"Why didn't you just tell me who it was?" Sarah

asked. "You had to have known, after what you and Merris did."

"After what Merris and I did?" He seemed genuinely confused, then his expression changed to one of disappointment. "You mean what I did to Merris? I knew you wouldn't solve it."

"What did you do to Merris?" Sarah was taken aback.

Arnie sighed heavily. "There was a lot I didn't tell you because I wanted you to work for it, for my house, by bringing my killer to justice. I appreciate your effort, but it wasn't Fred Williamstein who killed me."

Sarah gaped at him with mounting horror. "Arnie, did you steal Merris Golightly's treasure?"

He shrugged. "A small part of it. She couldn't have missed it. She found so much that she is probably still positively dripping in money. But she's a cutthroat one, and she can't let something like that go easily."

"Merris killed you? I thought it was a man?" She shook her head, amazed that she had been so wrong.

"It was a man. It wasn't Merris herself who stabbed me. But Merris had a way with men, and I'm sure it was someone close to her that she charmed into doing the deed." Arnie sighed. "I was even in love with her," he added with a surly grunt. "Everyone who met her loved her."

Sarah had even liked Merris on the phone. She was

horrified that her usual astute character discernment had failed. Furthermore, how had she been so certain that Fred was her guy? The vibes from him were definitely creepy, but it floored her that he wasn't the murderer she had been so sure he was. *Maybe I let my convictions get the best of me,* she thought. *And maybe Merris is just that good at charming people!*

"This information will help me," Sarah told Arnie.

Arnie grunted. "I don't have much hope, but all right."

CHAPTER FOURTEEN

AFTER THE MEETING WITH ARNIE, SARAH MET with her friends at Javacadabra, taking Addie along. She told them all on the phone that she had terrific news. She entered the coffee shop and beamed to see her coven and closest friends—Daisy, Frida, Margaret, Hua, and Susie and Karen standing behind the counter.

Without a word, she raised her hand and twisted it around so that the diamond ring on her finger glinted.

All of the witches erupted into cheers, clapping their hands with joy. Margaret and Hua ran to Sarah, enveloping her in bear hugs. So did Susie.

"He finally did it!" Frida cried.

"You already knew he would propose?" Sarah laughed. She thought back to the knowing looks that her friends had exchanged when she had mentioned moving in with Eli and Daisy's hint that he might be thinking something similar. Of course, they had all known. There was no sneaking anything past this bunch, not even a surprise proposal.

"He enlisted our help in picking out the best ring for you," Daisy said with a smile. "Men are generally clueless about these things, so he wanted to make sure he got something nice."

"Some of the rings he liked were hideous," Frida added dramatically. "I mean, they were pretty diamonds, but not elegant enough for Sarah Spellwood!"

Sarah started to cry tears of joy. "Well, you all did a great job. I'm in love with the ring, and I'm getting married!" She shrieked with joy and jumped up and down, her friends joining in. Even Addie jumped up and down and barked with excitement.

Zeva looked up from her nap on the counter and lazily blinked at everyone before groaning, "*Silly humans,*" and returning to her snooze.

"So when is the date?" Margaret gushed.

"We haven't set one yet," Sarah said.

"Summer solstice is always an opportune time to get married," Frida said. "It's when fertility is at its peak and the world is blooming. You should consider that."

"Whenever you set the date, we would love to help

you make it magical." Hua winked. "It's time for a proper witch wedding!"

"A proper witch wedding?" Sarah asked, intrigued.

"Of course," Hua said. "Every witch must be married in a special ceremony that prevents her husband from owning her powers. It also initiates you into a new state of being, as a married woman. And it helps Eli transition into married life, too."

"And we bring you so many blessings," Daisy added.

Sarah smiled. "Well, that sounds lovely."

"We have so many ideas to run by you," Daisy added, winking.

"And, boy, do I have a present for you," Frida chimed in. She reached into her satchel and produced a sheath of papers. "These are the property records for Arnie's house!"

Sarah gasped and accepted the papers. "What a sweet surprise, Frida. Thank you so much."

"Why didn't I think of that for a gift?" Daisy grumbled.

Sarah sat at the table, and Susie brought her usual green tea latte. As she sipped her drink, she delved into excited wedding planning with her friends. It felt nice to briefly forget about the murder mystery and the fight with Madras.

Finally, everyone had to go tend to different

responsibilities. They all hugged Sarah and congratulated her a final time. She smiled, watching her friends walk away, before gathering her things. "C'mon, Addie, let's go home and get some work done," she said.

"I'm so happy for you." Karen beamed from behind the counter where she was putting pastries into their neat rows in the display case.

"Thank you." Sarah smiled. "You, Susie, and Zeva are invited."

"*I hope so.*" Zeva purred contentedly.

Addie gave Zeva a threatening glance. Though she would never hurt Zeva, she also was not immune to Zeva's feline taunting. The two perfectly embodied the notion of "frenemies."

Eli's number showed up on Sarah's phone as she exited the coffee shop. "Hi, baby," she answered the phone.

"Well, we got a DNA sample from Fred and compared it to the blood samples from the crime scene that we still had stored in evidence. Most of the blood was Arnie's, but some of it wasn't. And, well, you won't believe the results."

"There wasn't a match," Sarah said flatly.

"There was not," Eli replied. "Hmmm . . . but it sounds like you already knew that."

Sarah sighed. "Try to run it in the database and see

if it matches anyway. Also, let's see if we can get a sample from Merris Golightly. Trust me on this one."

"I always trust you," Eli said. "I just can't wait to hear how you found this out."

"It's more than a lucky hunch, actually. Arnie came clean about a few things, and I'm confident Merris was at least partly behind it. I'm pretty sure the DNA won't match her, either, but maybe it will pull someone else up in the database. Then we can arrest them and find out how they're linked to Merris. Let's first rule her out completely as the killer, try to ferret out who actually did it, and somehow get a confession that Merris got him to do it."

"Wow. Okay, I'm taking notes here. I'll get on that."

"I was sure surprised to find out Fred wasn't our guy. I certainly didn't get a good vibe from him," Sarah added.

"Me, neither. He's definitely a bad guy, even if he isn't the killer. Well, don't worry, he will be doing some time. We're charging him with attempted armed residential burglary and breaking and entering," Eli assured her.

"Good," Sarah said.

"And, now, we have enough evidence to convince the district attorney to let us run the DNA through the database and try to find another match or a relative, like you suggested," he added.

"That's excellent news!" Sarah then told Eli she loved him and hung up. As she got to work for the day, she struggled to focus on the civil case she had to work on. She kept glancing at her phone, waiting for it to ring so she could learn the results.

Unfortunately, as Eli reported later when he came to bring her dinner, it could take up to a week to get the new results.

"In that case, let me show you the house," she told him enthusiastically, setting down her fork. "Arnie is a bit surly, so don't freak out if he throws a pebble at you or something."

Eli smiled a bit uncomfortably but agreed to follow her to the Victorian once they had finished eating.

They jaunted through Witchland in the gathering dusk, their arms around each other, huddled in their heavy coats. The trees were still bare, and the smell of smoke from woodstoves and fireplaces throughout the town hung tantalizingly in the frigid air. They finally reached the house, which looked especially naked and forlorn against the snow and the other beautifully painted houses in the neighborhood. From the street, Eli smiled up at it, shielding his blue, blue eyes from the setting sun.

What a beautiful man, Sarah thought adoringly.

"I like it," he said finally. "But it's going to need a lot of work. Do you even know if it's for sale?"

"I need to go to the library and find out who the owner is. I assume he would accept a reasonable offer for this place, considering that he isn't even using it for anything. Look, this maple is gorgeous, and we have a porch to drink tea and watch the passersby from. There's a huge yard in the back for Addie, and we can build a little doghouse for Kelvin to stay in when he visits. And a garage! Neither of us have any sort of cover for our vehicles right now," she said excitedly, leading him by the hand around the property.

Eli nodded. "And definitely more room. But remember, Sarah, we're both busy people. Will we really have the time to fix this place up?"

"Of course. We can work on it together, bit by bit, and stay in Michael's cottage until it's livable," she said happily. "Really, it just needs new paint, flooring, and a few new windows," she added. "From what I can tell, it's structurally sound."

Eli walked up to one of the windows and cupped his hands, peering through the dirty pane. "Looks like something hanging from the ceiling. I hope it's not the ceiling itself and just some drywall," he said doubtfully.

Sarah placed her hand on his back. "Baby, I know

we can do this. We love fixing and saving things. We love giving love. This house needs love."

Eli smiled slowly, nodding more and more enthusiastically. "Honestly, it was always my dream to find a nice fixer-upper to start my family in."

"So you will buy it with me?" she squealed, rocking up and down on the balls of her feet like a little girl who just found out she was getting a bike for Christmas. Her heart hammered with joy, and she wanted to shout how much she loved Eli and the idea of starting a family with him.

"Yes, I will," Eli promised her.

"You better solve my murder first or I will haunt you every day and make your lives miserable," Arnie's voice filled Sarah's mind.

"I'm working on it!" she told Arnie reproachfully. *"If you hadn't withheld important information, I could have solved your case much faster, instead of wasting time going after Fred Williamstein."*

Arnie did not have a reply. She could tell that he was sulking by the vibes she got from the house, however.

She couldn't wait to bring the angry ghost peace and help him let go of some of his rightful rage. She imagined living with him and Michael peacefully, a perfect blend of the living and nonliving dimensions in one home. Communicating with ghosts and living among them did not terrify her as it did other people; her psychic powers helped her see that they were not dangerous, but simply bent on achieving whatever they hadn't done in life. Of course, they had negative feelings sometimes, but that did not mean that they were inherently evil.

Just then, Eli's radio crackled. He turned the volume up and said, "Jenna, come through."

"We got a match," Jenna replied.

"Ten-four." Eli and Sarah exchanged excited looks before hurrying to the police station.

"I thought it could take weeks," Sarah said. "How did it happen so fast?"

"I pushed for the state crime lab to compare it to a few people that were central to the case. People the department had already interviewed in the eighties," Eli replied. "A few of them were actually in the database for other crimes, so looks like we got a match to one of them."

Breathless from running, they rushed into the humble police station. Jenna was at her desk, grinning. She handed them a fax.

Sarah leaned in to read the paper in Eli's hand. She gasped at the name printed under a grainy photo: John Golightly.

"Who is that? Merris's son?" Sarah asked.

"Ex-husband, believe it or not. Merris divorced him

sometime before Arnie's murder, but they continued to live together, and he lived with her when he was on parole in the nineties," Jenna explained. "He had been indicted in a voluntary manslaughter case in the early nineties and had served six years before getting out early on good behavior. Then he was suspected in another murder, but wasn't convicted, in 2009. That's how we have his DNA."

"This is certainly enough grounds for an arrest. Since he now lives in Tennessee, I'm calling the FBI," Eli announced. "I think we'll be able to get the truth out of him."

Sarah clapped her hands happily. "I can't wait to go back to the house and tell Arnie! His murder has been solved!"

She jaunted back to the house with the DNA results in her hand. Arnie did not say anything or even appear as she sat on the front step, but she felt his presence. "It was Merris indeed, or rather her ex-husband, who killed you," Sarah said out loud to the empty air.

"That good-for-nothing," Arnie spat, suddenly materializing on the step beside Sarah. "I should have known it would be her goon. That explains the weird voice. He had a voice changer and was always showing it off."

"Well, he's going to prison for your murder. But we're going to see if we can indict Merris based on his testimony," Sarah promised. "The grand jury trial is in May."

Arnie shook his head furiously. "They had better convict her! I detest that scheming woman."

"I wonder if Madras got the best of her and entered her, driving her to behave so greedily," Sarah pondered.

"It's just plain human nature," Arnie spat.

"It's not," Sarah assured him. "Not all humans are that conniving or evil."

"But most of them are," Arnie growled.

"I promise I will keep you updated," Sarah said, feeling uncomfortable around the vibes of Arnie's fury.

Arnie simply grunted. "That woman is slippery. She'll probably get out of it. Or run off to Mexico or something. I don't have much hope."

"Arnie." Sarah sighed. "You didn't have much hope that I would find out who did it, and yet I did. You really need to have more faith. We are doing our best."

"Yeah, well, try being dead and then tell me to have more faith," Arnie shouted. He then disappeared.

Sarah sighed, standing and tucking the papers under her arm. "I'll keep trying, Arnie," she told the empty space next to her. "I won't let you down."

CHAPTER FIFTEEN

THE RIBBON-CUTTING CEREMONY FOR THE NEW Witchland Visitor's Center and the naming for the newly acquired forest took place in the first week of May. Witchland had already awakened from winter and flourished early, as it always did under the tender care of the Leekins. Spring flowers burst from every inch, decorating the town and the forest in lively colors and cheer. Sarah was practically feverish with excitement for her upcoming wedding on June twenty-first and could not wait for the day to arrive, but now she had to shift her focus from wedding preparations to the ceremony. She had played a role in the acquisition of the land and had to take part in the ceremony along with the town's three mayors.

Under the guidance of its three mayors, Witchland had managed to generate the funds from renewed tourism to fill potholes and fix the library roof. More money was going toward new playground equipment for the city park, as well. But the most expensive purchase had been the land on the other side of Mount Katribus and the valley separating Mount Katribus from Blackberry Summit. They had also obtained a state grant to make it an official state park. The Witchland Forest had been increased by several hundred acres, acres that no one could develop now. Wildlife had even more protected space to flourish.

Sarah stood proud at the front of the brand-new visitor's center. The Mount Katribus trail system had been extended to reach into the new woods, and a small stone center had been erected at the very top, not far from the ghostly clearing. The hut contained signs educating people about the history and wildlife of the area. Beyond the center was a camping area that was designed to coexist with the trees so that none of them had to be cut down to make room for tents. The challenging and scenic hike and the camping area had already become renowned among outdoor enthusiasts who were eager to try it out, meaning many more tourists would come to Witchland to enjoy it and spend money in the town. Quite a few new faces were already in the crowd for the ribbon-cutting ceremony, having just completed the hike up Mount Katribus for the first time and bearing backpacks of camping equipment. They were eagerly awaiting the opportunity to explore the other side of the mountain and try out the new campground.

"We are pleased to announce the opening of the Mount Katribus Wilderness Area expansion!" Hua exclaimed to the crowd.

"And with that, welcome!" Malorie said. Wielding a pair of huge scissors, she snipped the red ribbon that Hua and Sarah had tied across the entrance to the visitor's center. The two halves of the ribbon drifted to the ground as people clapped and cheered.

"As always, remember to respect our forest and leave it the way you found it. If you pack it in, pack it out," Roger, the third mayor, declared. "Dead out campfires. Our woods are not at high risk of a forest fire, but they can and do happen. Motor vehicles are expressly prohibited, as is hunting and fishing. We are here to enjoy nature, not destroy it. There are trash cans all over the lower trails and the campground; please use them! If you want to use the campground, you have to book your spots online so that we know who is here and who is not supposed to be here. Your cooperation helps us keep this place nice."

"We also have a guest book for people to sign in and out of the trail at the beginning down in Witchland village proper," Malorie added. "That way, our park rangers can make sure people who went in came out. Because this is Witchland and strange things sometimes happen here, we will conduct search teams for people who don't sign out after twenty-four hours, unless they have purchased camping passes."

"We're officially a designated New Hampshire state park now, so this whole area is protected from hunting and development. That is a huge win for us and for our town!" Malorie declared. She was especially proud to have been instrumental in convincing the state government to declare the area a state park and the old Spellwood house ruins near the Leekins' fence a state historical monument. "But first we would like to present our one and only Sarah Spellwood with the key to the town of Witchland for all that she has done for us."

Sarah was starstruck. Even in her wildest dreams, she didn't expect this honor. But she had helped draft proposals, save the town from vindictive forces, and now she watched the ceremony with mounting joy and pride. The threat of greedy developers was gone, and poaching would be swiftly prosecuted. She had done her part in defending these woods. Tears of happiness welled in her eyes.

"Thank you all for this honor, I promise to always protect Witchland for many years to come," Sarah proclaimed.

Sarah smiled as people agreed to the rules without

anger, congratulated her, and began to stream into the center. It pleased her that so many people respected and loved nature as much as she and the other Witch-landers did.

"You did an outstanding job on this," Susan Lake said, stepping forward to congratulate the mayors and Sarah. "I'm so glad this finally happened."

"It was a process," Malorie admitted. "But so worth it in the end." She glanced at Sarah, her grateful expression saying everything. The woods were full of her family members, and now they were even safer.

"What do you say we go get our camping stuff and spend the night up here?" Hua suggested.

The other mayors and Sarah eagerly agreed. Sarah found Eli in the crowd and invited him to join her in her tent for the night. He agreed with a huge grin. They all climbed back down to Witchland to collect their things. Then they spent the night, roasting marsh-mallows and sharing ghost stories, around a huge campfire with the other campers. There were outdoor enthusiasts from all over New England, as well as a few German tourists, and Sarah enjoyed getting to know them. Their hokey ghost stories made her laugh.

When it came her turn to share a story, she smiled and said, "Let me tell you the story of Witchland's oldest ghost." Then she began describing Lativia Spell-wood, on her throne overseeing the forest, and her legions of faery helpers called Leekins. She then described Lativia's spiteful sister and archnemesis, Madras, and the epic battle between the two sisters at the top of Mount Katribus, not far from where the campground was located. She left out her role in the battle, giving all of the credit to Lativia, for the sake of privacy. But those who had actually been there smiled, knowing the real story. Those who had not been there gasped and stared, shivering inside their sweaters, thrilled by a fantastic ghost story.

Finally, John Golightly's trial took place. The recently cracked cold case had become famous throughout New England, resulting in a lot of news coverage. The news anchors credited the solving of the case to new DNA technology and the efforts of the Witchland Police Department, with no mention of Sarah. But Sarah didn't mind at all. She didn't want to have to explain to the disbelieving public why she had opened the case or how she could talk to ghosts. Eli attempted to convince her to take credit, but she always politely declined. As the trial began, Sarah and Eli got together to watch it on television.

Merris was one of the first witnesses. Sarah's jaw dropped at how lovely and poised Merris looked. She appeared as pleasant as her voice. With her perfect perm and sharp nails, she looked like any other well-dressed, well-coifed, and well-mannered lady. But as Sarah watched her, she was reminded more and more of a cat who had eaten the canary.

Merris swore on the Bible and then testified that she had some treasure that Arnie had stolen. She had no idea that John would kill Arnie over it, but she added that she wasn't surprised. She went on to spin a tale about how John had been abusive, threatening, and scary their whole marriage. "I left New Hampshire for California just to get away from the man," she said.

"That's not true!" John bellowed. "You cheated on me, and then you strung me along for years!"

"Order in my court!" the judge shouted, rapping his gavel.

John sat back down, looking red-faced and breathing heavily.

Merris appeared unruffled and survived the cross-examination without cracking. Some other witnesses were called to the stand by the prosecution, presenting more and more evidence implicating that Merris was lying about John, as well as her involvement in the murder. Merris's ex-daughter-in-law described Merris as manipulative and cruel. A former maid of Merris's stated that Merris had been the one to beat John, not the other way around.

Finally, it was John's turn to take the stand. With a shaky hand, he swore to tell the full truth and nothing but the truth. Then his attorney said, "Judge Harris, I wish to present to the grand jury a document."

"And what is the nature of this document?" Judge Harris asked.

"It's a letter from Merris Golightly to John Golightly, dated September 16, 1994, informing him about the robbery and insinuating that she wished him to do something about it. They had just been divorced, but there are a slew of love letters between the two that I will also present."

The judge nodded, and the attorney began a slideshow of the letters. The jury gasped as they read the obvious evidence. Merris still did not lose her composure, but Sarah imagined that her heart must have been racing.

Three hours later, the jury returned with a unanimously guilty verdict. Not only was John Golightly guilty, but so was Merris. Merris was arrested on both soliciting murder and perjury. John was sentenced to twenty-five years in state prison, Merris to fifteen. Sarah and Eli hooted with joy. "Considering their age, I doubt either of them are ever getting out," Eli noted.

Sarah went to Arnie's house immediately after hearing the verdict. She sat on the front step, which was clear of snow as it sat under the overhanging eaves of the porch roof, and waited. Soon, Arnie appeared next to her, looking anxious. "Well?" he said.

"Merris was convicted. She and John will be serving the last of their years in prison," Sarah informed him.

Arnie nodded, silent for a moment.

"How do you feel right now?" Sarah asked. The ghost was hard to read.

"I'm feeling . . . like I have only one regret in my life, and that was taking the treasure. I would rather be alive right now, enjoying tea on my porch, maybe a wife and maybe some kids and grandkids. Enjoying the connection with someone that you and Eli have," he said, glancing at Sarah. "I let greed get the best of me. We all did, Merris, Fred, Stuart, everyone in the treasure-hunting and gem-dealing crowds that I associated with. We all lived for the money and the thrill of the hunt. Except for John . . . John just lived for Merris. I knew it was dangerous, what I did, yet I still didn't expect to lose my life over it. It was foolish."

Sarah wished she could place a comforting hand over Arnie's, but she knew it would pass right through his transparent ghost body. "I'm sorry," she said softly. "But you have to let that regret go. It sounds like you lived your life to the fullest and did what made you happy."

"At the very least, I lived my life to the fullest," he

agreed with a solemn nod. "I did what I loved. I had adventures, and thrills, and fun." He turned toward her. "I want you to live your life to the fullest and appreciate every moment."

"Of course," Sarah said.

"I will now give you this house. Build the family you always wanted. Be happy every day. Now it's my time to cross over, but first I want to thank you," Arnie went on.

Sarah smiled slowly. "I was looking forward to living here with you, but I'm even more glad that you have the closure you need to cross over. If you are truly ready to let go, then I am here to support you. Don't be scared. You are not alone."

Arnie looked at her a final time, then glanced around his yard. He inhaled sharply, breathing in the scents of the world. He turned back to survey his home, probably remembering its former beauty under his care. Then he nodded with finality. Just as Sarah started to open her mouth to ask him what he was feeling, he started to shimmer, almost blindingly. Sarah shielded her face with her arm. When she peeked out again, Arnie had dissolved to a few sparkles, which soon winked out of existence. There was nothing in his place, not even the sensation of him.

Sarah glanced back at the house and realized that

its haunting aura of sadness and anger was completely gone.

She let out a long breath. Then she wiped her eyes, realizing that she had been crying. Sharing this beautiful, intensely intimate moment with Arnie and bringing him closure meant everything to her. *This is why I do what I do,* she thought.

She patted the step where Arnie had sat and then rose, dusting off her jeans. It was time to go home now.

Sarah finally scrutinized the property records for Arnie's house that Frida had gifted her. Arnie had been renting it to own from a Harold Palmer, but the property went back to Harold once Arnie died. Sarah eagerly called the Vermont number listed on the property records. After two rings, a man answered in a crusty voice, "Hello!"

"Hello, is this Mr. Palmer?" Sarah asked.

"Hello!"

"Mr. Palmer?!" She felt uncomfortable yelling into the phone, but she could tell the old man could not hear her.

"Yes! This is he!" the man shouted back, clearly unaware of how loud his voice was.

Sarah cringed and shrank back from the phone.

"This is Sarah Spellwood! I'm interested in your property at 805 Birdtail Lane in Witchland!" she cried.

"Who?!"

Sarah felt hoarse as she repeated her statement more loudly.

"Yeah? What about the place?" the man growled.

"I want to buy it!" she practically screamed back.

"Buy it?" He chuckled. "What, you want to tear it down, put up a Walmart there or something?"

"No! I want to fix it up and live in it! My husband and I." Sarah shuddered at the idea of erecting a Walmart where the beautiful old house stood.

"Live in it?" The man's voice sounded different now. "Honey, it may be a pretty old place, but I have to be honest with ya, someone died in there. And it wasn't a pleasant death—"

"Sir," Sarah interrupted, "I actually solved the case. I found out who did it. The people behind it are going to jail. You haven't been notified?"

"What?"

Frustrated, Sarah repeated herself, feeling her voice growing hoarser by the second. "Have you been notified?" Sarah shouted.

"Well, no, but I'm not the next of kin . . . Well, my, who did it?"

Sarah explained what had happened at the trial. She was surprised, since it had been all over the news, but Harold Palmer seemed like someone who spent his days fishing and not bothering with the news. After all, he was so hard of hearing that it was possible the television only annoyed him.

The man was silent for a long time. Then he said, "Well, let me see if my granddaughter will take me up there. I can unlock it for ya, let ya see if you really want to put any money into the thing. Let me tell ya, it is in rough shape!"

That weekend, Harold Palmer arrived in town with his granddaughter, Vanessa. He unlocked the house and stood on the porch with Vanessa while Eli and Sarah walked through it, admiring the beautiful curved banisters on the staircase, the dumbwaiter that still worked, albeit with some serious chain squealing, and the bay windows overlooking the tree and gnarled roses in front. Now that spring was flooding Witchland, the roses and tree were clothed in rich leaves that hinted at their potential beauty with some pruning.

"I think this would make a great office space for when I don't want to leave our home," Sarah commented as they surveyed the sun-filled parlor with the bay window. "And imagine coming in here for breakfast and tea on Sunday mornings," she went on, entering the cute breakfast nook overlooking the long-overgrown garden behind the kitchen. She opened a door into a shelf-lined pantry, imagining replacing the shelves strewn with rat droppings with new ones and filling them with her own canned and fresh produce that Margaret and Hua and other gardeners around town frequently brought her.

"This would be my man cave." Eli pointed out a little sitting room tucked past the kitchen. "And this could be our room," Eli went on when they traversed upstairs to the large master bedroom with its own bathroom.

"Maybe this could be a guest room," Sarah said, opening a door into a smaller bedroom with teddy bear wallpaper. Then she stopped, admiring what had clearly once been a child's nursery, probably even before Arnie had bought the house. "Or even a nursery?" Sarah ventured cautiously, unsure how Eli felt about kids.

Eli just grinned and put a hand on her back. "A little witch baby, or wizard baby. Can you imagine?"

"It'll be one cute baby." Sarah grinned.

Eli kissed her delicately on the lips. "I am glad you want a family. It's always been a dream of mine, to hear a little kid call me Dad."

Sarah's eyes grew moist. "I honestly never thought about it much. But now that you say that . . ."

They smiled at each other for a moment.

Mr. Palmer shattered the moment by shouting into the house, "Well?! Everything okay up there?!"

"It smells like mildew, but I like the place," Eli told Sarah, leading her by the hand down the stairs. They then stood in the center of the living room, looking around approvingly and nodding.

"You're really willing to take on all of this?" Sarah asked Eli.

"After saving Witchland five times from vicious magic, I must say that fixing up an old Victorian house doesn't seem so daunting," Eli joked.

They turned to face where Harold Palmer and Vanessa waited, peering at them through the open front door.

"We want it," Sarah said confidently, squeezing Eli's hand.

"You do?" Harold Palmer squinted at them with his watery blue eyes. "Well, how much you offering?"

"A hundred thousand, with twenty down?" Eli offered. He and Sarah had met the night before to discuss their finances and combined savings and had come up with their budget.

Harold laughed, a deep, hoarse sound. "Give me, oh, fifty thousand, and we'll call it even."

"Grampa!" Vanessa gasped. "You're just giving it away?"

"Not like you or the other kids want it." He shrugged. "I'm frankly tired of paying taxes on it." He turned to Eli and Sarah. "Murder houses don't sell, and Victorian houses aren't in. You two can make it a home. I live in a retirement home in Vermont, and I lost my Belinda years ago. I have no use for the place. And after what you did for ole Arnie, well, you deserve it."

CHAPTER SIXTEEN

June twenty-first arrived, and Sarah's stomach fluttered like there were a million butterflies taking flight all at the same time. She was not at all nervous to get married; the idea of spending the rest of her life with Eli was a dream come true. She also wasn't nervous about the wedding, which would include only friends and lovely magic ceremonies and blessings. But she was thrilled, and that made her unable to focus on anything. Life had turned into a wonderful dream for the past few years, and she could not get over how happy she felt.

Her wedding with Jeff had been big—and stressful. She remembered only feeling exhausted and eager to get the whole thing over with. Some friends of hers from law school had taken her out for drinks the night before, but it hadn't been a particularly fun night, and she had just wanted to sleep. It wasn't that she hadn't loved Jeff, because she had, but she had put more into the wedding than their relationship for months before the date. Looking back now, she noted that that was another mistake that led to the demise of their marriage, though things had obviously worked out in the end. This time, she was careful not to make that mistake and to keep the wedding all about her and Eli. Eli had been heavily involved in the planning process and had had a say in everything. It made the wedding feel like *theirs*.

But that night was all about her. Eli went to Buffalo for a little bachelor party thrown by a few of his friends and Lyle. Sarah's father, John, even joined them. Sarah stayed home, and her mother, Bernice, came into town to join the Wolf Coven sisters and throw Sarah a bachelorette party.

All of the women met at Sarah's cottage since Arnie's house was far from ready. Frida set out a stack of animal spirit cards and began to do readings on everyone. Margaret and Hua brought aromatic herbs that made Sarah's place smell lovely, and Susie and Karen brought treats.

"I'm so proud of my little girl." Bernice smiled over a glass of wine. "You have found the one, I must say."

Sarah beamed. "I sure did."

"And congratulations on that house!" Daisy spoke

up. "We'll have to go in and cleanse it and bless it for you."

"I think I effectively cleansed it." Sarah smiled. "But even though Arnie has crossed over, I would love my witches to do some deep magical cleansings."

Bernice looked confused. Sarah related the story to her, and she sighed. "I heard about that cold case being solved, and I should have known you had some hand in it."

"If you hear about any news coming out of Witchland, you know Sarah is involved." Daisy winked, and everybody laughed.

"I wonder what Eli is doing right now," Sarah said. "He promised none of those silly strippers," she added with a laugh.

"Whatever he is doing, he loves you fully," everybody assured her.

"Oh, it's not that I don't trust him. I just don't like him being so far away. We sure have gotten attached." Sarah laughed.

There was a strange ringing sound. *"Do you hear that?"* Addie asked Sarah.

"I do," Sarah said, glancing around to find the source. She didn't see anything, and the ringing only grew louder.

"Oh!" Bernice shrieked in surprise, knocking over her wineglass.

Sarah looked over and realized there was a Leekin hovering by her mother's ear, ringing a little magic bell made out of an acorn hat.

"Milo Figcreek," Sarah said, recognizing Clover Figcreek's brother.

Milo tucked the bell into the hem of his moss pants and pulled out a scroll. He unrolled it slowly and announced with great ceremony:

"Sarah Spellwood and friends, you are hereby invited to Leekin City for a night of feasting, dandelion wine, and celebration. We wish to usher you into your new role as the wife of Eli Strongheart, and congratulate you for your accomplishments in this town." His little voice filled the living room with surprising clarity.

"Oh, what is this?" Bernice laughed. "A Leekin party?"

"Welcome to Witchland once again, Mom." Sarah laughed. Then she turned to address Milo. "Of course, Milo Figcreek, we accept."

"Then follow me!" The Leekin's cheeks puffed out in pride as he led the women out of the cottage and into the woods, up to the Leekin fence. Addie bounded along behind them.

Once at the fence, Clover Figcreek flew out of a pine cone, screaming joyfully, "Aieeee!" Midair on his wings, Milo hugged her, squeezing her so tight that her tiny cheeks bulged out.

"Brother," she said. "I haven't seen you for two hours! It is good to see you!"

Sarah tried not to smirk at the silliness of the Leekins. Though she had gotten used to their oddities, they were forever a source of amusement to her.

The other Leekins flew out of their homes in masses. They swarmed the group of witches, each one shouting congratulations in what rapidly became a deafening cacophony of squeaking, trembling shouts. Addie whined, hating the sounds.

"We shall commence our celebration with a lavish feast," Clover Figcreek finally declared. The formality of her voice and its tiny shrillness made the women giggle.

Milo Figcreek nodded. He turned his back to the witches and spread his arms, uttering a string of Leekin-speak that the humans could not understand. Suddenly, they noticed the pine cones begin to rattle and shake. The trees began to change shape, looming larger and larger and receding in the growing distance. The blades of grass became as big as small trees clustered around them. The bark of the massive trees was filled with little golden orbs of light, illuminating the shapes of many more Leekins tucked away in carved holes. Great tendrils of vines began to curl through the air, linking together, forming bridges and walkways. Leekins streamed along them, sharing the walkways with ants, caterpillars, and grasshoppers. Two other Leekins rode a little golden leaf boat down a stream that trickled past Michael's glowing grave toward the fence and into a dozen more trees full of Leekin lights. Under the light of the moon that fell into a tiny clearing near the fence, a cricket played a tune by rubbing his back legs together, and a few young Leekins began to dance around it.

Sarah gaped at the spectacle. When she turned to look at Clover and Milo Figcreek, she was stunned to find she could look them in the eye. Addie still reached her knee and now was no bigger than some of the fat black ants in the plants overhead. The sudden shift in size had taken Bernice by surprise, but Sarah and the witches were not disconcerted. Nothing much surprised them anymore.

"Is this even real?" Bernice murmured, studying her hands and legs, then patting herself to see if she was dreaming.

"Need me to pinch you?" Sarah attempted to joke.

"Leekin City!" Daisy cried, flinging her arms and beginning to dance. "I always wanted to see this place! What an honor!"

"The honor is our gift to you, Sarah Spellwood," Clover Figcreek declared. It was a bit strange, to see her now level with them. She no longer needed to stand on a pyramid of her fellow Leekins to speak to them.

Margaret and Hua hurried into the vast city. Sarah, the other witches, and Addie chased after them. They followed Clover Figcreek into the clearing with the cricket, where she clapped her hands and called for her fellow Leekins to begin preparing a feast.

Using magic, the Leekins lowered several long sheaths of shed bark onto the ground and suspended them with magical ropes from the plants above. Others began to fly out of the holes in the trees, bearing huge plates of food and giant pitchers of glowing purple liquid that smelled like sweet wine. A young Leekin flew about, dropping little acorn hats onto the heads of the humans. Sarah giggled as a hat fell onto her head, feeling quite heavy for something so miniscule to her normal human size, and she gazed up at the happy young Leekin. "Thank you!" she said.

"Of course, Great Spellwood! You are our heroine! You all are!" the Leekin trilled back. Her cheeks glowed pink through the earthy brown of her skin.

"Enjoy your privileges as our honorary guests tonight!" cried Shamus Riverdasher. He clasped Sarah's face between his palms before kissing her cheek. Her skin glowed warmly where his lips had landed. "You take the honorary seat!" he said, ushering the humans and Addie to the head of one of the massive bark tables. The chair at the very head was shaped like a throne, and Shamus ushered Sarah into it.

Without further ado, Clover Figcreek rang a bell, and everyone began to devour what was in front of them. There were millet cookies, baked berry pies, chunks of honeycomb, and clover flowers soaked in apple juice. They seemed to consume only sweet things, Sarah noticed. Her mouth watered as the Leekins delved into the heaps of food. Unlike humans, Leekins did not observe any such thing as table manners. They seized food with their hands, stuffing their faces, then spoke with their mouths full as they haphazardly discarded stems, seeds, and husks onto the ground. They sloshed wine onto the tables and the ground as they cheered and tipped the goblets back into their mouths. Everyone wore food stains upon their faces and licked their sticky fingers. The feast tables were sources of great din. Sarah's ears rang with the roar of so many voices. She couldn't even talk to her fellow humans, but she communicated telepathically with Addie.

"What do you want to eat, girl? I'm sure you feel left out. There's no meat here," she asked.

"Some apple is fine," Addie responded.

Sarah reached for some apple on a dish formed out of a dried nonpoisonous toadstool, but Addie had other ideas. She leaped onto the table and seized some apple soaked in some sort of delicious spice and honey. The Leekins cheered for her, and she wagged her tail, beaming with her mouth full.

Sarah was about to admonish her, then relaxed. There appeared to be no special rules for politeness here. *"Did you know about this place?"* she asked Addie.

"The Leekins don't like to show their city to people. They mostly hide," Addie responded. *"But we familiars can smell all of this, so we know it's here."*

Sarah could not believe how much she was able to fit into her belly. She was positively ravenous, and just when she thought she was full, some more room seemed to open in her stomach. Finally, after a Leekin offered her a slice of red-and-white-spotted mushroom that was probably poisonous, she declared that she was finished in order to politely avoid eating it.

The other witches stared at her, unable to comprehend how she had eaten so much in such a short period of time. They had all thrown in the towel long ago. "You might regret that tomorrow when you try to fit into your gown," Bernice whispered.

Sarah wiped at her upper lip and smiled. "I don't think Eli will mind."

"Our guests are finished!" Clover Figcreek cried.

She sat on the other end of the same feast table as the miniature humans.

The Leekins rose from their seats on their wings. In a flurry of magic and frenzied activity, they began to disperse the dishes, all of which had been made from toadstool or woven from pine needles and could be safely discarded into the woods to compost into the rich topsoil. They tossed leftover food into the plants for birds, ants, and rabbits to enjoy. Finally, they lifted the tables off of their magical ropes and cast them away, to be used next time. The clearing was restored to its former emptiness.

Clover Figcreek began a long-winded speech about the Leekins' historical commitment to the forest, and their commitment to the Spellwoods. She spoke as if Lativia had only recently died, and Sarah wondered how long Leekins lived. When she asked a rather aged-looking Leekin near her, the Leekin only peered at her in confusion. "We live as long as we must," he said with a shrug.

"But how long is that? How many seasons?" she asked.

"I have lived through five generations of that tree," he finally answered after some thought.

Sarah realized that must be hundreds of years. "So you were alive when Lativia was alive?" she pressed.

The Leekin nodded, looking at her like she had a

second head. "Of course. Lativia is still alive and among us!"

Sarah sighed. The Leekins had a very dissimilar concept of time from her own. "How old are your children when they become adults, then?" she asked, observing a group of Leekin children ahead.

"As old as they need to be," he answered. Then he added, "My daughter first flew when thirty summers had passed."

Sarah shook her head, unable to understand exactly what that meant. She decided all she would ever know is that the Leekins were very, very old indeed. They had been bound to these woods for centuries, appointed guardians from before the arrival of the first Native Americans, as Clover Figcreek announced in her long-winded speech.

"Sarah Spellwood has blessed us with much help. She has defeated Madras once again!" she cheered.

The other Leekins raised their voices in joyful unison.

"Let's not focus upon Madras," she went on. "Let's be merry. And let there be no end to the dandelion wine!" She approached Sarah and draped a necklace carved from stone and studded with blue flowers around her neck.

Sarah touched the necklace lovingly. "I will cherish this," she assured Clover.

All of the Leekins cheered, and the witches clapped politely. Addie barked twice to show her happiness. Then some young Leekins came forward carrying more goblets of wine. Others began to dance to the rhythm of the cricket's music in the clearing where the feast had taken place moments before. A cicada and a frog joined in, and some Leekins started to play little instruments made of wood. One Leekin jigged in the center of the clearing, causing the little bells tied to his ankles and wrists to ring.

"Yoo-hoo! You two come on! We're about to have a ball!" Frida called.

Time became a blur as Sarah danced with the Leekins, her friends, and her mother. When she gazed up at the sky, overwhelmed by the large size of the moon, she only felt gratitude within her heart. "I'm about to be married!" she cried emphatically at one point, raising her fists in the air.

Daisy laughed and seized her waist, spinning her around the clearing.

"What—what happened?" Sarah groaned, cracking her crusty eyelids open. Addie was looming over her, licking her face. Something sharp was poking into her back.

Sarah bolted into a sitting position and felt her hangover headache crashing against her temples. She cried out and covered her eyes. Then she split her fingers and peered out.

All around the Leekin fence lay her friends. Bernice was curled up around a fencepost, lovingly holding on to the rotting wood with her fingers.

Sarah glanced behind her and saw that the sharp thing poking into her back was a broken miniature ring of some type, with blue flowers and stones. Vaguely, she remembered Clover hanging it around her neck last night. She realized that she had returned to her proper human size, judging by the scale of everything around her, and the necklace must have quickly snapped off of her neck when she grew larger. She slipped the necklace over her pinky and was pleased to see it fit snugly as it sealed itself closed around her finger.

"Sarah! You've been sleeping for a while! You need to wake up and start getting ready," Addie barked.

Recollecting the night before, Sarah shook her head. "Wow, we got wild." She crawled over to Daisy and shook her awake.

Daisy groaned and said, "I haven't felt this way since a wedding my mom's friend had in Haiti. I woke up on the beach, much like this."

Sarah moaned in agreement. "I haven't felt this way since my law school graduation night."

"Don't worry. I have a hangover cure in my shop," Daisy said.

They set about waking everyone up. Slowly, with many groans and whines, all of the women gathered themselves up and stumbled down the mountain with throbbing headaches. They crowded into Daisy's apothecary, where she offered them all thimble-sized cups of a golden elixir.

The elixir burned as it slid down Sarah's throat. Almost instantly, her headache cleared and her vision improved. She gasped. "I feel so much better."

"Good! Because you have exactly two hours to get ready now!" Addie barked.

Sarah gasped. "Oh, no. Mom, I really need you to run to my house and get my gown. Frida, do you have those hair clips you said I could wear?"

"Sure thing," Frida said. She shut her eyes, whispered a summoning spell, and the clips appeared in her palm.

"Can't you do that for your dress?" Bernice asked, clearly not ready to run to Sarah's cottage yet. Her hangover was lifting, but not quite.

Sarah smiled and tried a spell that she thought would work. Her gown suddenly appeared, hovering in the air by Daisy's counter.

"Only the best for our favorite witch," said Daisy as she fondled the glittering pearls and Swarovski crystals that appeared to be the color of the sun. "This gown sure shows your witch heritage. And this little golden veil will look divine with your hair. And the color is your favorite—forest green. Oooooh, I am so excited."

"It is utterly perfect," Sarah agreed dreamily. "Thank you, everyone."

Jenna appeared a few moments later with her makeup kit. While the other witches helped Sarah into her gown and fixed her hair with flowers, enchanted star-shaped lights, and Frida's clips, Jenna began to do her makeup. Finally, she handed Sarah a mirror. Sarah gasped. "Oh, my, I look like a woodland faery princess," she said.

"Just what you wanted, right?" Bernice smiled. Then she clapped Sarah's face in her hands. "I just want to say I've never seen you so beautiful, and I am so proud."

"I love you so much, Mom. All of you." Sarah hugged Bernice and then everyone else in her circle. "Thank you," she told them.

"Ready?" Daisy asked.

"I've never been more ready for something in my life," Sarah said.

With the help of her friends holding up her train, Sarah made her way up the mountain to the new visitor's center. There, she saw that her friends had magically set up chairs and a wedding arbor draped in floating enchanted flowers.

"This is a good luck fetish, from voodoo culture," Daisy said, fixing a strange-looking doll on the side of the arbor. "It will ensure that evil cannot ruin your marriage."

"Thank you," Sarah said. Then she turned at the sound of people entering the area from the trail. It was Eli and the other men. At the sight of him in his suit, her heart rose into her throat and tears of joy misted her eyes.

CHAPTER SEVENTEEN

Hᴜᴀ ʟɪᴛ sᴏᴍᴇ ᴡʜɪᴛᴇ sᴀɢᴇ ᴀɴᴅ sᴍᴜᴅɢᴇᴅ ᴛʜᴇ aisle. Eli and Sarah then followed her to the arbor, where Daisy now stood with a special book. Eli and Sarah stood before Daisy, holding hands. Off to one side gathered Michael, Sarah's father, and Lyle; on the other side stood Addie and Kelvin, each holding a red rose in their mouths. In the front row sat Bernice, Ruth, Frida, Margaret, and Hua, all dressed in white robes.

"We are gathered here today to witness the union of Eli Strongheart and Sarah Spellwood," Daisy began.

Sarah was surprised to hear the ceremony commence in such an ordinary way. She had expected it to be a bit more mystical.

But her expectations were soon met. Daisy began to read the next verses in Latin and threw out a handful of ashes from a basket set beside her. Instead of settling to the floor, the ashes sprang up into a large shower of sparks that then began to mingle and form the shape of a long-tailed bird. Sarah gasped when she realized the bird was a phoenix. Eli stared, his mouth hanging open, as the phoenix flew into the air and turned to survey them with its blazing eyes. Its tail streamed behind it, white and pulsing with power. Then it gradually diminished into fiery sparks.

Ruth started in her seat. "What kind of firecracker was that?" she frantically whispered to Bernice.

Bernice smiled at her mysteriously and said, "A Witchland kind."

"Let this phoenix become a spirit animal for your marriage, which will symbolize your love and devotion," Daisy said, switching back to English. "You will always cherish each other, never forsake each other, and never forget each other's best interests. You live to better one another, not to quarrel or bicker or live in division."

Margaret rose and tossed a handful of salt between Eli and Sarah. The tiny white granules settled, dusting their clothes. "Let this salt cleanse you of your past baggage and allow you to join in holy matrimony as pure beings," Daisy recited.

"And let these two candles symbolize your status as separate beings, one in life but separate in body and soul. You walk the same path, but you do not meld into one being," Daisy read on. She lit a candle and used it to light another on the little table where their marriage certificate waited.

Hua stood and took the roses that Addie and Kelvin held. She tossed them over the couple, and the petals showered down gradually. "Let these flowers symbolize the beauty you both share and the admiration you share for each other. Let that not turn into jealousy, or a fight for power, or ugliness of any kind," Hua said.

Sarah felt tears spring into her eyes once again.

"May you drink this mead to celebrate your love for each other and for Mother Nature," Daisy went on.

Frida brought them shot glasses of mead. Sarah and Eli linked hands and took their drinks.

Daisy snapped the book shut. "Now, have either of you prepared vows?"

Sarah began to recite a medieval love spell to Eli, though she did not put any magic behind it because she knew she did not have to. Their love was strong, and everyone around them could feel it. Her heart hammered as she looking into his eyes. Placing a hand on his wrist, she saw a single tear flowing down his cheek.

Eli took a breath and adoringly looked into Sarah's eyes. "Sarah, until that day I first laid eyes on you, I was just living my life, going through the motions. Sure, I was happy with my job and my life here, but I knew there had to be more. I just didn't know what it was—until I saw you. Then it all made sense. You make me complete."

Exclamations of "aww" came from the crowd, and Addie barked. *"Oh, please,"* Kelvin said as he rolled his eyes, but Sarah could tell his heart had secretly melted, too.

"Does anyone have any objections to this couple joining together with the blessed elements of earth, wind, fire, and water as their guides in marriage?" Daisy called.

No one stirred or said a word.

"Are you sure? We all know how terrible these two are together," she joked with a wink.

Again, no one said anything.

Daisy slid the wedding certificate toward Eli and Sarah, along with an inkpot and a quill. And as they signed the license, a beautiful blue light radiated from the quill. Sarah gasped. "Oh my stars! How beautiful." She looked at Eli and giggled as she intertwined her hands with his.

"By the powers invested in me by the state of New Hampshire, the divine forces of nature, and as a High Priestess, I now pronounce you lawfully and spiritually wed! You are joined now beyond love and into the heavens. You may now kiss," Daisy said with a mock flourish of the pen as she added her own signature.

Eli gently caressed Sarah's cheek, then placed her veil over her head and kissed her. Literal sparks flew through the air, and everyone gasped as they began to cheer and clap. They began to throw birdseed at the happy couple. A sudden twinkle caught Sarah's eyes, and she pulled away from Eli to look up. A Leekin was flying overhead, dropping a shower of twinkling, enchanted stars over the couple.

"It's for good luck and eternal happiness!" cried Clover Figcreek. Sarah realized that the Leekin queen was hidden within the flowers at the bottom of Addie's flower girl basket.

Blackberry Hoppers began to spring across the entire clearing around the visitor's center, the sun glinting beautifully off of their metallic grasshopper-like bodies. Sarah smiled and gazed past them to some movement in the trees. She felt her heart swell when she realized the movement belonged to the two bear cubs she had helped save, who were romping in the brambles, Miwak watching over them. They had gotten so big. Miwak raised a paw toward Sarah before leading her cubs off into the darkness of the trees.

Sarah laughed out loud before kissing Eli again. Then, as they began to walk down the aisle, everyone rose, clapping. Everyone except Ruth, who remained in her seat, looking stricken at the magic she had just witnessed. Michael patted Sarah on the back, knowing that only a few people could see him, and told her, *"Good luck, my fabulous Sarah. I'm so proud of you. Tell Eli he had better take care of you because an over-protective ghost is watching!"*

Sarah whispered what Michael had said to Eli. Eli grinned. "Of course, Michael!" he said aloud, not at all ashamed to embrace the reality of magic and ghosts.

Ruth was still staring at them with her eyes wide. "I think you should get your mom," Sarah whispered to Eli. "This introduction to magic may have been a bit much for her."

Eli ran to his mom while Sarah's parents hugged her. Then her friends joined the hug, forming a massive group hug.

The reception in the town square was so full of people and food that Sarah didn't know what to do with herself. It seemed she had to be in a million places at once. Everyone had brought presents, and there was an overflowing pile near the long potluck table. Sarah wondered where she would find room for all of the gifts in her new house, though she was also very grateful. A DJ from out of town, hired by Malorie as a wedding present, played great music, including some of Sarah's and Eli's favorites. She and Eli barely got any chance to dance, though, because they were so busy receiving well wishes and congratulations from everyone.

Sarah finally felt a hand on the small of her back, and the hairs on her arms stood on end. "Michael." She beamed at the ghost of her mentor.

"Dance with me," he urged.

She let him take the lead, and they began dancing in the center of the town square, the only place big enough in the town for the massive reception. People gaped, then looked away, shrugging. "She's a Spellwood; what can you expect? Of course there would be some kind of magical mumbo jumbo," they all seemed to agree without any judgment. They did not bother her, letting her be in peace for this one dance. Most people understood she was probably dancing with Michael Howler, whom they all missed as well.

"I just want to tell you how proud I am of you, of the life you've made." Michael tucked some of Sarah's hair behind her ear in a loving, fatherly gesture. *"You made this town what I always dreamed it could be."*

Sarah beamed. *"You made my life what I always wanted it to be, even though I didn't even know it yet. I feel complete."* She looked down at Addie, who wagged her tail happily and followed the dancing pair in circles.

She tearfully finished the dance with her beloved mentor and returned to her husband and friends. Daisy wiped her tears away and hugged her.

"Sarah," someone said coolly behind her.

Sarah turned to see her mother-in-law standing there. "Ruth," she said happily.

"That was quite a spectacle," Ruth said wryly. "I knew there was something odd about you, and now Eli has explained things—well, things I'll never understand."

Sarah smiled and placed a comforting hand on Ruth's shoulder. "Spend enough time here, and you will get used to it."

Ruth shook her head. "I just can't believe it. Everything I knew about life has been challenged."

"I know how you feel because I felt the same way when I moved here," Sarah affirmed. "But trust me, it gets better."

"Well, I must say, you look lovely. Your wedding was not my taste, but I can respect it," Ruth said. "I am glad you two found each other. And best of luck on your new house."

Sarah beamed. "Thank you."

Ruth nodded a bit dazedly, clearly still in shock from all she had seen and learned that day, then moved away to speak with Bernice. The two women seemed to hit it off and spoke for most of the night after that.

Sarah started at the sound of a whistle and then a burst. It was a firework, unfurling in yellow and gold across the sky over the town square. It was now finally dark, and fireflies flashed among the trees. Some kids began setting off more fireworks. The music stopped, and everyone stood in the center of the square to watch the spectacular lights.

"What a special day," Eli murmured, taking Sarah's hand. "Things got a little wild last night, and you won't believe what a partier Lyle is. It blew my mind. I have a hangover, I have to admit."

Sarah laughed. "I did, too, but Daisy has some great stuff for that."

"I need to hunt her down and get some, but I just want to enjoy this moment with you." Eli smiled.

Sarah smiled back at him, then returned her gaze to the light spectacle above. "I love today. And I love you. And I will love you always."

CHAPTER EIGHTEEN

THE MONTHS AFTER THE WEDDING WERE peaceful, beautiful ones. Sarah and Eli set to work on their new home in the evenings after work, peeling the water-stained wallpaper from the parlor in the front. They began to tear up the linoleum on the floors, which was yellowed, peeling, and littered with rat droppings and accumulated filth from forty years of disuse. They replaced the hanging ceiling in one of the rooms and some of the broken windows. The wood was still in good shape, and they began sanding it. They had spent all of their savings on the house, and since Sarah had been working much less since moving to Witchland, she did not have much left in the bank. They couldn't afford a contractor, but they didn't mind. Working on the house together felt like making their dreams come true.

Wiping sweat from her brow one day, she sat on her heels while Eli heaved up a layer of linoleum and gasped in dismay. They surveyed a massive layer of mouse droppings underneath. He groaned. "This is going to be fun. This place is hazardous, Sarah. I wonder if we made a mistake." The look of discouragement on his face broke Sarah's heart.

"I have an idea," Sarah said suddenly, grinning mischievously.

"Uh-oh, what are you going to do?" he asked. He knew that look meant she had a trick up her sleeve.

She winked at him before muttering a spell under her breath. The mouse droppings suddenly disappeared and were deposited far away in the woods, where they could return to the earth and fertilize plants. Any diseases that they may have carried were also removed from the home, leaving it safe and clean. Sarah laughed and brushed her hands together. The floors now looked spotless.

"Are you serious?" Eli gazed at her, a playful smile tugging at his lips. "You mean to say you could've been using magic this whole time?"

Sarah nodded. "It's definitely an option." Then she giggled at the mock anger on Eli's face.

"You've been holding out on me!" Eli exclaimed.

"I felt it would be cheating!" Sarah laughed.

Eli playfully threw a scrap of wallpaper at her.

Thereafter, Sarah used her powers to clean the house up and swipe away strips of wallpaper, flooring, and old paint. She even transformed the old wallpaper in the nursery into fresh wallpaper with daisies, and convinced the beautiful wood fixings, trim, and wainscoting to regain their former highly polished glory. When they decided to completely remodel one of the bathrooms and expand the kitchen, she did both jobs in record time, costing them almost no money at all, save for the cost of the new fixtures and tiles.

Eli did some work, laying down tile and carpet, replacing the windowpanes, mainly to keep up appearances and save Sarah some energy. It did wipe her out, focusing so much magical power on the house. Eli also needed to feel that he was doing his part in creating a home with his life partner for their future family. Sarah thought about how intimidated he must be of her powers and smiled, relieved to have found a man who accepted her just the way she was without resentment.

When it came time to paint the exterior of the house, Sarah waited until midnight in the middle of September, when they were already nearly finished with the interior. Addie stood at her side while Sarah shut her eyes and willed the old paint away, replacing it with bright yellow paint and handsome green trim. The house instantly looked cheerful, almost like an entirely new property.

Addie gasped. *"I can't even see color, but I can tell it looks nice!"* she said. *"The wood just looks more uniform and even, and there's something brighter about the place!"*

Sarah nodded. "Amazing what colors and fresh paint can do for a house."

———

"It's truly amazing how fast your contractors painted your house. You got them to work overnight?" Susan Lake exclaimed at Javacadabra the next morning.

Sarah just smiled secretively at her coven sisters, who hid their smirks behind their cups or napkins. "Yes, they're the best in the region! Very expensive."

"You'll have to give me their number!" Susan said.

"Sure thing. I'll have to find it first," Sarah told her. As Susan walked away, she began to giggle with the other witches. "Home improvement for under ten grand." She winked.

"So many perks to being a witch." Margaret sighed happily.

"Isn't it nice to be using our powers for nice things? Instead of battling Madras?" Daisy said happily, sipping her tea. "I'm really enjoying developing new potions with hoodoo elements from my background."

"I've been working on deciphering an ancient cuneiform spellbook," Frida piped up.

"And we just got some exciting new magical plants for our greenhouse," Hua said, exchanging thrilled glances with Margaret.

"I sense Madras might still appear again," Sarah said. "It seems like just a part of our lives now. But we'll never give up defending this place. It's our home!"

"For now, dear, just focus on your marriage and your new home," Daisy told her lovingly. "We'll all take care of the rest when it comes."

Moving day came with a splash of fall color as September drew to a close in Witchland. Sarah stepped into the new home she would now share with Eli, carrying a heavy box of her files. She lovingly glanced around and breathed in the lovely scent of fresh paint, new carpet, and polished old wood. The odor of mildew was gone, and everything cracked and broken was gone, too. The house's aura of trauma and sadness had become one of gentle cheer and happy expectation for the future. She set the box down in the parlor that she intended to turn into her new office and met Eli back outside to unload some furniture from the moving van.

Addie barked and ran around outside, chasing her tail. "Silly girl," Sarah told her, laughing.

"*I'm just happy,*" Addie barked joyfully.

"Here's the kitchen stuff." Eli handed Sarah a big box.

Sarah accepted the box. It was surprisingly light, suggesting how little they cooked. Sarah planned to change that. She carried it into the kitchen and began to unpack. As she knelt to place a pot in one of the bottom cupboards, she noticed a deep crevice between the boards at the floor of the cupboard. *Strange,* she thought. *I repaired these cupboards with magic, so Eli and I never actually investigated them in person. I wonder if this is a little compartment to hide something in?*

She found a large knife in the box and slid it into the crack. With a jimmying motion, she worked the floorboard up. Then her breath caught as she saw what lay underneath.

"Eli!" she shouted.

Eli hurried into the kitchen. "What's wrong?" he gasped.

"Look." Sarah held up two heavy gold bars. "I guess Arnie didn't hide all of his treasure in the woods."

Eli gasped and knelt next to Sarah. He reached into the compartment and pulled out another gold brick. "Look at this!" Turning the brick, he showed Sarah the inscription carved into the metal.

To Eli and Sarah. Best of luck. Arnie.

Sarah began to tear up. "Oh, Arnie. I miss his cantankerous presence! I always knew he had something very good in his heart."

Eli pulled Sarah close to him. "Looks like we'll be set for a while. What should we spend all of this on?"

"A college fund for any kids we have, and something really nice for Witchland," Sarah told him.

He grinned and began to cover her face in kisses. "I think that's a great idea."

All was well in Witchland.

Would you like to be notified of the next book in The Spellwood Witches series?

Get Notified Here!
https://wendyvandepoll.com/melanie-snow

A NOTE FROM MELANIE

Ms. Addie Pants and I came across a real mama bear on Mount Katribus. Didn't have time to take a photo!

Thanks so much for reading this book. I love how Sarah has come into her strength with her witchiness. Don't you?

This story was special to me as I have had numerous wild bear encounters. And they always taught me patience, perseverance, and survival. Addie and I even had a meeting on top of Mount Katribus.

Sarah's journey with discovering her lynx, wolf, crow, fox, and bear medicine is powerful medicine and I hoped you found kinship with her. If you didn't read Witch's Tail, Book 1 please start from the beginning to experience her full adventure.

Here is a sneak preview of book one in the series, *Witch's Tail*, which is now available on Amazon. Here is the link to skip the preview and read the whole magical book. http://getbook.at/witchstail

Did you enjoy Pawtrayal?

Just in case you didn't read Book 1

Get Witch's Tail Now

http://getbook.at/witchstail

Witch's Tail

The Spellwood Witches, Book 1

Can she awaken her dormant powers and stop a desperate killer destroying the forest?

Sarah Spellwood feels she's hit bottom. Divorced and jobless, she relocates to the enchanting village of Witchland intent on solving the murder of her late mentor. But as she pursues clues buried in the man's fight to save the endangered forest-dwelling lynx, she makes an enemy of a ruthless land developer.

Encountering faeries in the woods, Sarah discovers she's been repressing unique gifts passed down from her ancestor and founding witch, Lativia Spellwood. But though she can now hear her deceased friend's dog speak, she isn't sure her abilities are enough to expose the greed and corruption covering a killer's lies.

Can Sarah work with the magical beings to bring a murderer to justice?

Witch's Tail is the charming first book in the light-hearted The Spellwood Witches cozy mystery series. If you like paranormal puzzles, delightful canine companions, and environmental enlightenment, then you'll love Melaine Snow's wagging-ly fun whodunit.

Buy Witch's Tail to set a snare for an assassin today!

http://getbook.at/witchstail

ENJOY AN EXCERPT FROM WITCH'S
TAIL

Do you want to know how Sarah got to where she is now? Or what about Addie: what is her magical journey? If you are started with book 5, Pawtrayal you will be able to find out in the first book of the series: Witch's Tail!

Witch's Tail is now available on Amazon. Here is your link to get your copy right now!

http://getbook.at/witchstail

You're not ready to get your own copy? Enjoy part of the first chapter for free on the next page!

Witch's Tail
Chapter 1 . . . in part

New York City top real estate attorney. Fierce redhead with green eyes. Direct descendent of Lativia Spellwood, a survivor of the Salem Witch Trials and the most notorious witch legend in New England. Sarah Spellwood was all of those things, and she thought she had life all figured out, until it fell apart before her very eyes.

The problems all started when the man Sarah had married ten years earlier approached her one evening after she got home from her law firm. Jeff looked at her with his steely gray eyes, not a hint of a smile on his smooth shaven face, and asked her for a divorce, plain and simple. His tone of voice sounded as if he was asking her where she wanted to go out for dinner. He then walked out the door without a hint of an explanation.

A few days later, his best friend, Lance, showed up. Sarah opened the door, curious to see him. "Is everything okay?" she asked.

"Yeah, I'm just here to get Jeff's clothes," Lance replied. He looked apologetic and wouldn't quite meet Sarah's eyes.

"Why is he doing this?" Sarah begged Lance.

Lance only looked at her with sympathy before sharply looking away. He shrugged. "He just said the spark is gone. I'm sorry, Sarah."

"Is there someone else?" she demanded.

"I don't think so. You know Jeff isn't that kind of guy. I really don't know anything else, or I would tell you." Lance shrugged apologetically again and went about boxing up Jeff's things.

There was no fight, no anger, no rebuilding the relationship, no marriage counseling. They had originally met in the quad of law school and had gone through late-night study sessions, finals crunches, bar exam anxiety, and friend drama together. Getting married had been an obvious choice, as they were best friends. Though work had often come between them over the past ten years, Sarah thought their marriage had been sound. They'd always been able to talk about their problems—analyzing and discussing before things got out of hand. But this was different. He simply walked out.

One of the main things Sarah loved about being a lawyer was the fact that she loved to talk and work things out. She had learned to separate her emotions from the facts early in her career and that had carried over into her married life whenever things got too heated between her and her husband. So why couldn't she get him to talk this time? And where had their love mysteriously gone? Surely there was another woman, but Sarah couldn't find out anything.

Sarah finally got a clue during the divorce proceedings. Jeff had filed on grounds of irreconcilable differences. He didn't speak to anyone unless he had to. Even her commanding green eyes couldn't get a rise out of her husband like they had in the past. But when the mediator asked him what he wanted of their shared assets, he snarked, "She can give me a lot more than this; Lord knows she makes more money than I do. She's always bragging about winning this case or that one." Then he glanced at her, his eyes blazing with hurt pride.

Sarah gaped at him. "Is that why you're doing this? Because I'm a better attorney than you?"

He refused to look at her or answer, telling her that she had guessed the reason. Recollections of his silence when she talked about winning a new case, the times he complained she didn't make him dinner because she had been late at the office, and even the times he grumbled that men teased him at his firm about how they ought to fire him and hire his wife instead, came tumbling back to her. How had she missed it after so long? She was normally so intuitive, yet with her own marriage, she had missed the signs.

So, Sarah gave him everything but the apartment, and he didn't contest that at all. It was clear she just wanted to be done with it all, to go start her new life. She heard he moved to Chicago shortly after the divorce and took a job at a new firm, where no one knew how talented his ex-wife was with real estate law.

As she trudged through the annoyance of changing her last name back from Lawrence to Spellwood, and enduring the excited looks from people who wanted to know if she was related to the infamous Lativia Spellwood, her hurt soon became replaced by a hot coal of rage that burned inside her heart, a sense of betrayal and a misguided rejection of love. As a Lawrence, she had been proud, and she had been able to avoid the looks and questions that had haunted her all of her life thanks to the Spellwood name. Now, she was single, thirty-five, and getting the looks and questions again. "So are you related to Lativia Spellwood?

GET YOUR COPY NOW!

http://getbook.at/witchstail

DISCOVER
THE SPELLWOOD WITCHES SERIES

WITCH'S TAIL, BOOK 1

Can she awaken her dormant powers and stop a desperate killer destroying the forest? If you like paranormal puzzles, delightful canine companions, and environmental enlightenment, then you'll love Melanie Snow's wagging-ly fun whodunit.

Here's the link to buy the book today!
http://getbook.at/witchstail

HOWL PLAY, BOOK 2

A novice witch. A collie companion. Can this clever duo put noses to the ground to chase down a killer? If you like cute flirty romance, discovering one's true destiny, and love for animals, then you'll adore Melanie Snow's barking-ly fun adventure.

Here's the link to buy the book today!
http://getbook.at/howlplay

TAIL OF A FEATHER, BOOK 3

A mysterious portal. Eight crows with a message. A missing police chief. If you like paranormal puzzles, charming canine companions, and a bit of flirty romance, then you will love Melanie Snow's crafty quest. Take flight into the magical world of Witchland.

Here's the link to buy the book today!
http://getbook.at/tailofafeather

IMPAWSIBLE MISCHIEF, BOOK 4

Stolen charms. A mysterious woman running for mayor. Can beginner's magic save an ill-fated land? If you like wisecracking creatures, enchanting characters, and close-knit sisterhoods, then you'll love Melanie Snow's clever story.

Here's the link to buy the book today!
http://getbook.at/impawsiblemischief

PAWTRAYAL, BOOK 5

When a ghost cries murder, an unsolved case could cost her future. Can this witch solve the magical mystery when an old enemy starts casting chaos. If you like wise familiars, heartthrob romances, and mystical whodunits, then you'll love Melanie Snow's paranormal brainteaser.

Here's the link to buy the book today!
http://getbook.at/pawtrayal

Don't Miss Your Free Gift!

Thank you for purchasing *Pawtrayal, The Spellwood Witches, Book 5*. To show my appreciation and because of a popular request from my readers
I am offering a:

Welcome to Witchland Map
https://wendyvandepoll.com/melaniesnowgift

Join Melanie Snow's Paranormal Cozy Mystery
Facebook Group

The Wolf Coven
https://www.facebook.com/
groups/melaniesnowcozymysteries

About Melanie Snow

Melanie Snow is the pen name for Wendy Van de Poll, a bestselling author, pet loss grief coach, and animal medium. She is the author of The Spellwood Witches, a paranormal cozy mystery series.

Her books weave together positive magic, snarky forest faeries, and insightful animals with fun and eclectic humor. True life adventures and intuition are woven into her stories laced with unbridled imagination.

She has been followed by wild wolves in minus sixty degrees, hissed at by a mama bobcat, and played ball with a wild owl—among other animal encounters.

Find out more about her work by visiting her on her website: https://wendyvandepoll.com/melanie-snow and also get *The Welcome to Witchland Map*.

Download Your Free Gift
https://wendyvandepoll.com/melaniesnowgift

HOW TO FIND MELANIE SNOW

www.wendyvandepoll.com/melanie-snow

www.facebook.com/melaniesnow.cozymysteries

www.instagram.com/melaniesnow.cozymysteries

www.facebook.com/
groups/melaniesnowcozymysteries

www.amazon.com/author/melaniesnow

www.goodreads.com/melaniesnowcozymysteries

ACKNOWLEDGEMENTS

I would like to thank my intuitive writing team who has guided me to write this fun series. They weren't always easy to deal with but they were patient with my fumbling. Because of them Melanie Snow and all the characters in my head have come to life.

I appreciate all my teachers of the furred, feathered, and finned variety who continue to guide me through life and teach me what matters.

A special thanks goes to my weekly writing buddies H.R. Hobbs and Toni Crowe who are kind, sassy, and amazing authors.

I offer a tremendous amount of appreciation to my beta readers: Nadine, Vicky, and Renee. To my editor

ACKNOWLEDGEMENTS

Robyn Margaret Verdugo a huge thank you for your expertise. And thank you to my talented proofreader Allison Rose.

A huge hug goes to my husband, Rick Van de Poll. He is a remarkable poet and human being who dedicates his life to the animals and the environment. He inspires my soul. You can find his books on Amazon, as well.

And of course, Addie. This rescue puppy flew on a jet plane from Texas to grace my life in many ways and writing books with her as a main character is just one. Addie even has her own series called; The Adventures of Ms. Addie Pants on Amazon.

CPSIA information can be obtained
at www.ICGtesting.com
Printed in the USA
LVHW100309120922
728134LV00015B/66

9 780578 839912